BETTY WALES
DECIDES
A STORY FOR GIRLS
by
MARGARET WARDE

AUTHOR OF

BETTY WALES FRESHMAN
BETTY WALES SOPHOMORE
BETTY WALES JUNIOR
BETTY WALES SENIOR
BETTY WALES B. A.
BETTY WALES & CO.
BETTY WALES ON THE CAMPUS

ILLUSTRATED BY
EVA M NAGEL

Introduction

BETTY WALES and her friends appeared first in " Betty Wales, Freshman," which told the story of their freshman year at Harding College. Eleanor Watson was in that group; so were Mary Brooks, Helen Adams, Roberta, the three B's, and Katharine Kittredge, of Kankakee. Madeline Ayres made her entrance in " Betty Wales, Sophomore." " Betty Wales, Junior," and " Betty Wales, Senior " completed the undergraduate history of Betty's class. " Betty Wales, B. A." is the story of a summer abroad, where Betty met Mr. Morton, and " Babe " met his son. " Betty Wales & Co." described the beginnings of the famous Tally-ho Tea Shop, and " Betty Wales on the Campus " brought Betty back to Harding as the Secretary of the Student's Aid Committee. She lived in Morton Hall, erected by the testy old millionaire because Betty's work had won his sympathy and interest.

The " ploshkin " referred to in this story

was at first a fascinatingly impossible little animal in a story that Eugenia Ford told Betty's Smallest Sister, but Madeline Ayres saw its wide possibilities as a fun-maker, and Jasper J. Morton helped the girls put images of it on the market.

Contents

Illustrations

Betty Wales Decides

Betty Wales Decides

CHAPTER I

IT was a breathless August afternoon. Betty Wales, very crisp and cool in white linen, sat in a big wicker chair on the broad piazza of the family cottage at Lakeside. On the wicker table beside her were a big basket of family mending, a new novel, and an uncut magazine. In her lap was a fuzzy gray kitten. Betty Wales was deliberately ignoring the mending; she had been "perfectly crazy" to begin the new novel, but now she ignored that likewise; she had entirely forgotten the fuzzy gray kitten. She was busily engaged in the altogether delectable occupation, for a hot August afternoon, of doing nothing at all.

Jim Watson,—Eleanor's brother, you remember, and the architect in charge of Morton Hall, also a warm admirer of Morton Hall's pretty little manager,—had been in Cleveland for a week "on business." The business was connected with two big houses that his firm were building there. It had left all his evenings and most of his afternoons wholly at the disposal of the Wales's family cook, alias the pretty little manager of Morton Hall. The cook had rushed through her work in a scandalous fashion that caused the Wales family to indulge in many loud complaints of too-early breakfasts, "snippy" lunches, and wildly extravagant dinners—Jim always got out to Lakeside in plenty of time for the dinners. He had left for New York the night before, after the very most elaborate and delicious dinner of them all, and the Wales's family cook was tired, though she did not know it, and happy, in spite of a queer lonely sensation that was hopelessly mixed with relief at having a long, lazy afternoon all to herself, to spend with a kitten for company, a book for diversion, and plenty of mending in case the unwonted joys of idleness should pall.

At four, when the postman came by on his

afternoon round, Betty was still staring absently off at the blue lake, thinking vague, happy thoughts. She was so absorbed that she never even saw the postman, who obligingly walked across the piazza to her corner and dropped the afternoon mail in her lap, right on top of the gray kitten, who was too sleepy to care.

Just one letter, and it was for Miss B. Wales, the address typewritten, the name of Jasper J. Morton's world-famous banking house in a corner of the envelope. It was from one of Mr. Morton's secretaries,—not the Harding graduate that Betty had sent him, but an energetic young man who had been with the firm for several years. It was he to whom Mr. Morton had delegated the task of marketing ploshkins in New York and elsewhere, and he and Betty had become quite friendly over the checks and reorders and other business arrangements.

"I regret to state," he wrote now, "that the ploshkin market has slumped. Our regular customers all report that they are 'stuck,' to use a technical expression of commerce, with the ploshkins they already have on hand, that the demand has entirely dropped off, and that they do not anticipate a revival of it.

"Mr. Morton has asked me to communicate with you, expressing his regret at the sudden termination of so profitable a business. (You will be amused, I know, to hear that the first thing he said was, 'My, but that relieves my mind. It always worried me to think of people wanting to waste their money on those silly old splashers.')

"Fortunately the spring sales used up practically all the stock you had on hand, so there will be no losses to meet. But there will also, I fear, be no more profits.

"Mr. Morton respectfully suggests that the ingenious young lady whose name he is unable to recall shall coöperate with you in inventing a new specialty. 'Most anything will do if it's only silly enough,' in Mr. Morton's opinion ; and he will gladly arrange to market the product as he has the ploshkins.

"Hoping anxiously for such a renewal of our business relations, I remain,

"Most respectfully,
"Samuel Stone."

Betty laughed heartily, all by herself, over Mr. Morton's characteristic remarks. It was fortunate, she reflected, that when he was cross he was always comical. Otherwise she would never have made friends with him in Europe, and then he would never have built Morton Hall at Harding to please her, nor helped the Tally-ho Tea-Shop out of its very worst trouble,—nor sold the ploshkins. She smiled all to herself at Mr. Samuel Stone's " anxious hopes," and frowned as she contemplated the utter impossibility of making the ingenious young lady (named Madeline Ayres) invent a new " specialty " except by some such happy accident as had produced the ploshkin, that comically sad little creature, with an " ingrowing face " that smiled, a prickly, slippery tail, and one wing to hide behind, plaster images of which had been circulated, by the energy and enterprise of Jasper J. Morton and Samuel Stone, from New York to San Francisco, if not further.

And having laughed and smiled and frowned, Betty read the letter all through again, sat up straight in her big easy chair, and, choosing one of Will's stockings, began to darn the very biggest hole in it. She wanted to think hard, and she could always think harder when her fingers were busy.

A slump in the ploshkin market meant no more ploshkin income. When she considered staying at home for the winter, Betty had counted on that hitherto prolific source of revenue to keep Dorothy on at Miss Dick's, as well as to provide herself with necessary pin-money. Father wanted her to stay at home, but Betty wondered sadly if he realized how much she would cost! A girl doesn't know about that until she has tried living on her earnings. Betty Wales understood just how fast little things will count up, try as you may to be careful. Father wasn't yet back on Easy Street; Will had made a bad joke to the effect that Easy Street was certainly Hard Street when it came to getting a place on it again after you had carelessly slipped off.

"That's true as well as funny," Betty reflected sadly, "and the reason is that people who have been rich don't know how to be poor. We're still an extravagant family, no matter how hard we try to save. So I almost think—oh dear! I wonder if they do miss me much at home when I'm away! Because President Wallace is sure that Morton Hall will miss me if I don't go back to it. I wonder if he's right. I almost think —— Goodness, I should hate to seem conceited about it, because I know as well as anything that it's perfect nonsense the way they all think I can do things that other people can't. Anybody could do anything that I've ever done,—if they'd only try," ended Betty Wales, with a fine disregard for antecedents and a serene lack of appreciation of the rarity of people who try—and who keep on trying to the bitter end.

If Dorothy didn't go back to Miss Dick's there would be two extra ones at home ; that would put boarding, with five in the family, out of the question, and rents in town were frightfully expensive. It did seem as if a person who had a good salary waiting for her in Harding would better "go back on the job," as Will would have put it.

A big, snorting motor-car slewed round a corner, with a silvery peal of its "gabriel," glided swiftly down the street, and drew up with a lurch in front of the Wales cottage. Betty, her eyes on Will's stocking, her thoughts working hard on the perplexing Harding-or-no-Harding problem, gave a little start at discovering that she was going to have callers. By the time she had dropped the stocking and carefully arranged the kitten in a comfortable little furry ball on a hammock cushion, the two ladies in the tonneau of the car had shed their protecting goggles, hoods, veils, and ulsters, and started up the path to the door.

"Nobody I know," reflected Betty, going forward hospitably to meet them. They were both young—more likely to be Nan's friends than Mother's, and Nan was off spending a week with Ethel Hale Eaton. Looking more closely Betty decided that they must have mistaken the house; the pretty, overdressed girl with the huge plumed hat, and the more subdued young woman in a wonderful silk gown and a close-fitting toque, both in the very latest style, did not look quite like friends of Nan or indeed of any of the Wales family.

The girl was ahead as they came up the steps. "Is Miss Wales at home?" she asked in a sweet, assured voice, smiling a dazzling smile from beneath the big drooping plumes.

"Do you mean the real Miss Wales—my sister Nan?" Betty asked. "She's away paying some visits. I'm Betty, the next youngest. Won't you sit down a moment?"

"Thanks, yes," the older woman, with the sweet, subdued face and manner answered. "And it ain't your sister we want. It's you. I'm Mrs. James O'Toole, of Paris, France, and that's my girl Marie."

"I'm very glad to meet you both," Betty stammered. "That is,—I haven't met you before, have I? I have such a bad memory."

"No, you haven't met us," Miss Marie O'Toole told her with an amused giggle. "If you had, you'd remember. Even people with bad memories don't forget Ma and me."

"No?" Betty laughed back at her in friendly fashion. In spite of the plumes, too much jewelry, and an absurdly hobbled skirt, there was something very winning about Miss Marie O'Toole, with her pretty doll face and her sweet, thrilling voice. But Mrs. O'Toole was a curiosity. Betty had had to try hard not to jump when the demure little lady, dressed with such exquisite elegance, had opened her mouth and been suddenly transformed into a very ordinary person with a dreadful twang in her voice and a shock-

ing lack of grammar in her conversation.
She listened in blank silence to her daughter's
comment, and then handed Betty a card.

"That's to interduce us. Has the letter
followed?"

Betty stared in bewilderment. The card
was President Wallace's, introducing Mrs. and
Miss O'Toole. "Letter will follow" was written after the names.

"Oh," exclaimed Betty comprehendingly,
"you are friends of President Wallace's, and
he is going to write me about—something.
I'm very glad to meet any friends of his.
Isn't he splendid?"

"I think he's a cross old bear," returned
Miss Marie O'Toole sweetly, "and Ma thinks
he hasn't ordinary common sense, don't you,
Ma?"

"Never mind about that," said Mrs. O'Toole
sharply. "But we ain't any friends of his.
The letter to follow is about Marie entering
the college. I told you we had ought to have
waited a while, Marie, for that there letter."

Marie smiled blandly. "Oh, I don't know.
I guess we're capable of explaining ourselves
to Miss Wales."

"I'm sure you are," agreed Betty hastily. She was bursting with suppressed curiosity.

"Well," began Mrs. O'Toole, "it's like this. Marie wants to go to college. I can't think why, but she does. She met some swell New York girls in Paris last winter, and they told her that it was all the rage. Of course," added Mrs. O'Toole magnificently, "we know all the elect of the American colony."

"She means élite," explained Miss Marie with a giggle. "Hurry up, Ma, and get to the point of your story."

Mrs. O'Toole sighed a patient, long-suffering sigh and continued. "So when we came across in June, Marie went right up to Harding and took the exams, and she failed in most of 'em. So then she was more sot than ever on her idee, and she hired a teacher to travel with us all summer—a girl that this President Wallace recommended. And last week she tried again and done better, but not good enough to suit."

"The tutor was so tiresome," explained Miss Marie with asperity. "She told me that I couldn't possibly pass, so of course I couldn't. Go on, Ma."

"So then she was still more sot to go," went on Mrs. O'Toole, "and she sent her Pa a tellergram and he——"

"You can't toll that part," broke in her daughter hastily. "Don't you remember that he said not to—President Wallace, I mean?"

"Well, anyhow, nothing come of it," said Mrs. O'Toole wearily. "But he finally sent us here, to say that if you'd undertake Marie she could come, otherwise not. She'll be terrible disappointed if you won't," ended Mrs. O'Toole, "and if you will she's willing to pay quite regardless."

Marie giggled nervously. "That sounds as if I was buying a hat, Ma, or an invitation to an exclusive ball. President Wallace said that money was no object to Miss Wales."

Mrs. O'Toole glanced sharply at the little cottage and then at the perfectly plain white dress that Betty was wearing, with its marked contrast to Marie's furbelows. "Money is something of an object to any sensible person —except some college presidents," she added pointedly.

Miss Marie O'Toole turned to Betty with a

pleading smile on her pretty face. " I guess you understand what I mean," she said, " and please do say that you'll ' undertake ' me."

Betty looked perplexedly from one to the other. " But what am I to do ? " she asked. " I don't understand what you mean by that word."

" There ! " exclaimed Mrs. O'Toole triumphantly. " I told you we had ought to have waited for the letter."

Miss Marie shrugged her shoulders impatiently, and turned to Betty. " President Wallace said that he was willing, under the circumstances —— " Marie hesitated. " I suppose he meant my being educated mostly in a convent, where they don't prepare girls for college, and being so ' sot ' on coming, and so on. Anyway he said that under the circumstances he was willing for me to enter with one more condition than is strictly according to rules, if you would promise to tutor me as you did another girl once, and to look after me generally, and explain things that I don't know about. He said he thought I would find a lot of things at college that I didn't know about."

There was a long pause. Of all the embarrassing situations, Betty thought, this was the worst. President Wallace was—it would be very disrespectful to say what. Besides, Betty realized in spite of her annoyance that President Wallace undoubtedly had had a good reason for sending the O'Tooles out to spoil her lazy afternoon. Part of the reason was probably because he had had to send them somewhere, or he would have them still pleading with him to reconsider his decision. Betty foresaw that Marie, being "sot," would not give up easily; while Mrs. O'Toole, wanting Marie to have what she wanted, would be equally persistent. Betty decided that she needed a breathing space.

"I don't know what to say," she told them. "To begin with, I haven't fully decided to go back to Harding this winter. If I do go, I shall be very, very busy with my regular work. I don't really see how I can do more than I have already arranged for. But before I decide, I must wait for President Wallace's letter. It may be about you, or it may be partly about Morton Hall—the dormitory that I shall have charge of if I go back. May

I have a little time to consider? I really couldn't say anything but no, if I had to decide to-day."

Mrs. O"Toole sighed and looked reproachfully at Marie. "I told you so," she complained. "You're always in too much of a hurry. We might just as well have taken things easy and enjoyed the ride. We came all the way in our car, Miss Wales."

"But I like to ride fast," announced her daughter calmly. "Do you, Miss Wales? Because, if we're going to wait around here for that letter, I'll take you for a ride. Do many Harding girls have their own cars?"

Just then Tom Benson appeared on the piazza. Betty presented him, and Marie promptly dazzled him with her smile and bore him off to a distant corner of the piazza.

As soon as she was out of ear-shot, Mrs. O'Toole leaned forward in her chair and addressed Betty earnestly. "Do it if you possibly can," she begged. "It's a foolish notion she's got that she wants to go to college, but there ain't anything bad about it. It ain't as if she wanted to go on the stage, or ride bareback in a circus, or marry some good-for-noth-

ing fellow that wants her for her money. So
I'm awful anxious for her to have her way.
You see, Miss Wales, I know I stand in her light
some. I know I ain't a lady, though I do dress
perfect," she added proudly, "and look so
young that people are always asking Marie
about her pretty older sister. But looks and
money ain't everything, Miss Wales. And
Marie is always so awful nice to me and her
Pa, that we aim to suit her as well as we can."

"Did Mr. O'Toole come to America too?"
asked Betty, for want of anything better to
say. She couldn't help being touched by
Mrs. O'Toole's plea, but she didn't want Mrs.
O'Toole to know it yet.

"Oh, he's always in America," explained
Mrs. O'Toole, "out at the mine, you know.
But that's no place for Marie, and her Pa
knows it. He wants her to have all the bene-
fits of education and foreign travel. We
ought to be going, Miss Wales. Day after to-
morrow, did you say? All right. You've
been awful kind, Miss Wales. Come, Marie,
we must be going."

Marie came, slowly and reluctantly, with a
backward smile for Tom Benson, and a mur-

mured, "To-morrow afternoon then, and we're staying in town at that big hotel with the queer German name."

Betty watched them go as she might have watched the curtain dropping on the last scene of a tragi-comical play. Tom Benson broke into her revery with a laughing comment.

"Your friend Miss O'Toole is an accomplished little flirt, all right," he announced.

"She isn't my friend," Betty told him severely, "and it takes two to flirt, Tom Benson. So, as a favor to me, you're not to call on her in town. You can come over here and see her day after to-morrow if you want to. It looks to me as if I had been tumbled into the job of chaperoning her through the first half of her freshman year at Harding, so I propose to start her out right."

"Why the first half of the freshman year only?" demanded Tom curiously.

"Because," explained Betty, "mid-years come then—at Harding. Seems to me I have heard that they come about the same time at Yale, but I suppose they don't worry a distinguished scholar like you."

"The fair Marie doesn't act particularly studious," admitted Tom. "But you can't ever tell about these pretty college girls." Tom smiled meaningly at Betty, for whose brains he professed a vast admiration.

"Well, I wasn't flunked out at freshman mid-years," Betty told him, "but if I didn't think Miss Marie O'Toole would find half a year of Harding all she wants, for one reason or another, I certainly shouldn't be contemplating acting as her special tutor."

"Are you considering it?" demanded Tom in amazement.

Betty nodded calmly.

Tom whistled. "Then I bet you have your hands full."

"Well, I certainly hate having them empty," returned Betty, beginning again on the stockings.

CHAPTER II

BETTY WALES always insisted that the O'Tooles' visit had nothing whatever to do with her decision to go back to Harding.

" I see through you, Mademoiselle," Will teased her. " You think you'll be getting ready to be married about next year, and you're taking your last chance to say a long farewell to your beloved Harding,—also to save your three-decker, secretary-tutor-tea-shop salary for a grand and elegant trousseau."

" Will Wales ——" began Betty fiercely, and then relasped into haughty silence (accompanied by the faintest blush) as the only proper treatment of such unfounded accusations.

Nan was amused, and Dorothy relieved, of course, that her favorite sister was to be within call again. At first Mr. Wales agreed, rather soberly, that it would be foolish to neglect such good opportunities ; but before she left home

27

Betty had made him laugh so heartily at a few of her pet business theories, mostly adapted from Mary Brooks Hinsdale's Rules for the Perfect Tea-Shop, that he accepted her decision as a huge joke—just another of Betty's whims, having no painful connection with the ebb of the family fortunes.

But Mother, with the illogical perversity that is proverbially feminine, took the amazing position, for her, of Marie O'Toole's ardent defender and champion.

"If you're not going back chiefly on that poor child's account," she told her daughter Betty, "why, I'm ashamed of your unsympathetic nature. I never was so sorry for any one"—she had been present on the occasion of the O'Tooles' second call. "She's so sweet and pretty,—and so ignorant of all the things that other sweet, pretty girls learn from their mothers. She must know how strangely Mrs. O'Toole strikes nice people, but she doesn't act annoyed or embarrassed, or try to keep her mother from making those dreadful remarks. Mrs. O'Toole says that they have never been separated, and that she doesn't know how she can live next winter without Marie."

" Betty thinks they can safely prepare for a grand family reunion after mid-years," laughed Will.

"And then," explained Betty practically, " I can have time enough to do justice to Morton Hall and "—very mysteriously—" to a lovely new plan that I have for the Tally-ho. Of course, as long as I'm going back anyhow, I won't be mean enough not to ' undertake ' Marie. But I hate having a lot of entirely different things to be responsible for, and I specially hate tutoring. I only hope this girl won't cry all the time the way Eugenia Ford used to. It was fearfully embarrassing."

" Tom Benson advises you to make her join an anti-flirt society first off," Will put in solemnly. " He says it's lucky Harding isn't a co-educational college, because in that case it would take about two able-bodied chaperons to look after the gay Miss O'Toole."

" Tell Tom Benson from me that I'm glad he's at Yale instead of Winstead," Betty retorted loftily. " A girl who wants to go to Harding badly enough to study all summer, take two sets of exams, and enter with three conditions hanging over her, isn't as silly as Tom Benson seems to think."

"Certainly not," Mother defended her oddly-chosen favorite. "President Wallace must have seen her possibilities, or he wouldn't have asked Betty to help her out. He evidently feels just as I do about her. I am sure that she has a naturally fine mind, and that she will respond very quickly to the cultivated atmosphere of the college. I doubt if Betty will need to do more than give her the most casual sort of instruction."

Betty smiled to herself in the sheltering darkness of the piazza, where the family was spending the evening. Her private opinion coincided closely with Tom Benson's, to the effect that even without the complications of co-education, Marie would be "a handful." But President Wallace had hinted that he had a good reason which he was "not yet at liberty to communicate" for asking Betty to try to get Marie creditably through her freshman year; and, as Betty put it briefly to herself, it would be mean, just because it meant hard work, to refuse to do what the tragi-comical O'Tooles had set their hearts on.

So that matter was settled. The Students' Aid work had developed so rapidly that Betty had petitioned for a senior assistant, and also, to the vast amusement of the Association's managers, for a smaller salary for herself. Betty was bent on securing enough leisure to carry out her "lovely new plan" for the Tally-ho. Jim Watson may have had something to do with her feeling, or he may not; but, for one reason or another, Betty had what Madeline Ayres called a "leading" that this would be her last chance at Harding ; and she wanted to "finish out" the Tally-ho, partly because she wished Mr. Morton to feel fully justified in his purchase and improvement of the property, but chiefly just to satisfy her own queer little sense of the fitness of things. The Tally-ho was capable of more than had ever yet been developed; and Betty liked people and institutions to do their very most and best. But the details of all this planning were kept a grand secret, even from the Smallest Sister, who had been the "Co." in the Betty Wales business firm. Betty wanted to look over the situation at Harding first ; then she would be ready to confide her conclusions to Co., Babbie and Madeline.

Betty Wales went back to Harding three days before the college opened, in order to get a good start with her work. But almost before she had stepped off the train she found herself up to her neck in a deluge of Students' Aid affairs, all marked "immediate," at least in the minds of the persons most concerned. It was a large factor in Betty's success that she could always get the other person's point of view ; but there are occasions when this trait makes its possessor very uncomfortable. Betty wanted every girl who had applied for the Association's help to get it, if she was worthy ; she wanted every lonely freshman to be met at her train, every boarding-house keeper in search of waitresses, and every well-to-do student who hated to do her own mending, to feel that nobody could supply their varied wants so well as the Students' Aid. The result was that one small secretary was shamefully overworked, almost forgot that she was supposed to be helping to run the most successful tea-room in Harding, and had no time to spend in worry over the probable bothers connected with tutoring Miss Marie O'Toole.

President Wallace was of course infinitely

busier than Betty ; all he had found time to do about Marie was to tell Betty, with a twinkle, that he had perfect confidence in her ability to manage " even the extraordinary product of a mining camp, a convent in Utah, a Select School for Wealthy American Girls in Paris, and the companionship of Mrs. James O'Toole; and to transform said product into a freshman that should be a real credit to Harding College."

Whereupon Betty had gasped at the complicated things that were expected of her, laughed because President Wallace was laughing and seemed to expect that of her too, and then hurried off to find Miss Ferris and ask her if Mary Jones, the senior who lived in an attic at the other end of High Street, couldn't somehow be persuaded to pocket her pride and come to fill an unexpected vacancy in Morton Hall.

She painstakingly met the train that Marie had written she would take ; though either Marie had missed that train or Betty missed Marie. But with the capable assistance of Mary Brooks Hinsdale and Helen Adams she found Rachel and Christy, and Georgia Ames and Eugenia Ford found her. And the six of them, declaring that she looked tired to death and almost, if not quite, starved, bore her off to the Tally-ho for refreshment.

"Which is the biggest, most comfy chair you've got, Nora?" demanded Mary. "Bring us tea and the best little cakes you have for seven."

"Better make it for fourteen, Nora," amended Georgia. "I'm fairly hungry."

And while the seven ate for fourteen, they all talked at once of "wonderful" vacations, "dandy" trips, "thrilling" summer adventures, each story ending with a rapturous, "And now aren't we having a grand time here?"

"I must go and find that freshman," Betty declared at last. She had said the same thing before, but this time she meant it.

"No, you mustn't," Georgia told her firmly, tumbling little Eugenia into her lap as a precaution against sudden flight. "You must tell me where she boards, and I'll go and dry her tears, help her to unpack, explain about morning chapel and freshman class assembly, and tell her to meet you in—let me see—oh, the note-room in the basement of College Hall, at eleven o'clock sharp. She's sure to be through by that time, and if you're busy then, why, she can just wait for you."

Betty listened to Georgia's program in obvious relief. "Oh, Georgia, would you really do all that? You're an angel! With so many other things on my mind, having to hunt her up seems like the very last straw. But Georgia—she's—rather queer—not like other girls, I mean. She's lived abroad a lot and her mother is—peculiar." Betty tried to forewarn Georgia without prejudicing the company against the absent Marie.

"Don't you worry, dear," Mary Brooks Hinsdale reassured her. "Georgia will manage your freshman. Miss Ames, I hereby rechristen you Georgia-to-the-Rescue, and elect you to take extra-special care of our precious Betty Wales."

Georgia blushed very red at being praised and "elected" to a mission by the charming Mrs. Hinsdale. "I don't care how queer Miss O'Toole is," she declared stoutly. "I guess I can make her understand a few simple messages. I've wanted to see the inside of that elegant new freshman hotel-affair where she's staying. Go to bed early, and get rested, Betty dear."

When the college clock began to strike eleven the next morning Betty reached for her rain-coat—the freshman downpour had duly arrived—to run over to College Hall and keep her appointment with Marie. But she had pulled on one sleeve, when Miss Ferris appeared to say that she had interviewed Mary Jones, who lived at the other end of High Street, and had persuaded her—it took fifteen minutes to tell what. Just outside Betty's door Miss Ferris encountered Georgia Ames, red and panting. Georgia skilfully avoided a collision, slipped inside Betty's office before the door had fairly closed upon the departing Miss Ferris, and dropped, breathless, into a chair.

"I thought maybe you'd forgotten your freshman," she panted. "So I came to remind you. Don't know why I hurried so. Only—she is entertaining the whole note-room, and it's full of girls, and she is just screamingly funny, Betty, though I shouldn't say so to any one else. But some of the other girls will pass on her choice remarks—the grind book will be full of her. And I couldn't help liking her last night, so I thought I'd better come and remind you." Georgia paused awkwardly.

"You know she just happens to be my freshman," Betty explained smilingly. " I was asked to tutor her and look out for her a little. I liked her too, the little I've seen of her." Betty had slipped on her rain-coat while they talked. " Come and help me find her, Georgia-dear-to-the-Rescue."

The note-room is a notable Harding institution, time-honored and hedged about with inviolable customs. It gets its name from the four letter-racks, one for each class, that cover the long wall opposite the windows. The other walls are patched with Lost and Found and Want signs, and with notices of class and society meetings. A long table runs almost the length of the narrow room. On Mondays the janitor piles upon it the week's accumulation of dropped handkerchiefs, for their owners to claim and carry off. On other days college celebrities may sit on it, swinging their feet comfortably while they beam on their admirers or wait to keep a "date" with one of their "little pals." It is unwritten law that no freshmen save only the president, vice-president, and Students' Council member may sit, or even lean, on the note-room table.

The note-room is always crowded between classes, and on this first disorganized, rainy morning it was a favorite rendezvous. As Betty and Georgia wormed a slow passage through the crowd near the door, they could see Miss Marie O'Toole, dressed, quite without regard for the weather, in a furbelowed silk gown, a huge be-flowered hat, and—of all things at Harding !—gloves, perched comfortably on the sacred table, between Fluffy Dutton and a clever little sophomore named Susanna Hart. Fluffy was all smiles and attention ; Susanna's black eyes twinkled with suppressed glee. Around the table surged a mob of girls, all amused but the freshmen, who were deeply and seriously interested in what was going on.

"Yes, I think I shall like it here," Marie was saying in her sweet, piercing voice. "It's so friendly and informal—not a bit like Miss

Mallon's Select School ' pour les Americaines ' in dear old Paree. I've talked to lots of nice girls this morning. I can't remember half their names, but they nearly all promised to call on me. You will too, won't you?" She beamed impartially on Fluffy and Susanna.

"Maybe, if we have time. Got a crush yet?" inquired Fluffy sweetly.

"A what?" Marie's face was blank.

Fluffy explained.

Marie giggled consciously. "You embarrass me, Miss Dutton. You go off and stand in a corner of the hall for a minute, and I'll tell the rest of these girls whether I've got a crush or not,—and what her name is."

Fluffy slipped obediently off the table, and then pulled the amazed Marie roughly after her. "Freshmen aren't allowed on this table," she announced sternly. "You'd better go home and read the rules of this college. There's a rule about crushes, too. And about asking upper class girls to call." Then tender-hearted Fluffy relented and held out her hand. "I must go now," she said. "But it won't be against the rules for me to call on you, and I will. Where do you live?"

Marie explained, her gaiety somewhat subdued. Just then she caught sight of Betty
and Georgia, who had at last succeeded in getting somewhere near the sacred table.

"Oh, Miss Wales," she cried eagerly.
"Here I am, and I need your help right
away. Where can I find a set of the college
rules—about calls, and crushes, and sitting on
tables like this one, and so on?"

"And passing exams in freshman math.,"
murmured Fluffy wickedly, hazarding a guess
that Marie's brain was not of the exact, scientific variety. "How do you do, Betty? I'm
coming to the Tally-ho for tea and a talk to-
night—Straight too. You'll be there?"

Betty said yes, trying to look properly reproachful and not succeeding at all. Meanwhile the crowd had drawn back, old girls
having whispered to the gaping freshmen that
Miss Wales was a "near-faculty."

"Shall we come over to my office?" Betty
suggested, nodding right and left to girls she
recognized. Marie covered her silken elegance
with a natty white polo coat, and thoughtfully insisted on carrying the umbrella over
Betty on the way back to her office.

"Just look at that, Miss Wales," she began, as soon as they were seated, handing Betty a printed list of the accepted freshman candidates. "I'm in. I wouldn't believe it till I saw it down in black and white. And I'm the only O in a class of two hundred. Isn't that funny, Miss Wales?"

Betty looked sympathetically at the name of the only O in the freshman class. There it was, down in black and white: Montana Marie O'Toole.

"Oh, how f——" began Betty, who was fast being overwhelmed by the accumulating absurdities of her protégée. "Why, I—I thought Marie was your first name."

Marie giggled. "I'm always called Marie—now. Ma would be awfully mad if she saw that ridiculous old Montana cropping out again. But they told us, when I took my first exams, to put down our full names. I asked if 'M. Marie' wouldn't do, and the teacher in charge of the room just glared at me ; so of course I wrote it all out in full about as quick as I could. You see, Miss Wales, I was born in a mining camp, and Pa named me after the claim where he'd struck it rich the

very day I came into the world. The Montana
Mary it was called. When I went to Salt
Lake to school I dropped the Montana, and
when I went to Paris I changed Mary to
Marie. Marie suits me better, don't you think
so, Miss Wales?"

Marie got up to shed her heavy polo coat,
and stood, a dazzlingly pretty vision, smiling
down at Betty with the half-pleading, half-
commanding curve of her lips that made her
so winning in spite of her crudities.

Betty smiled back at her. "You'll be
Montana Marie as long as you stay here," she
told her freshman. "So you'd better make
up your mind to it. The girls always seize
upon a queer name and use it. If you'd written just Marie, you might have been nicknamed something funny ; so it would come to
the same thing in the end. Now may I tell
you a few things, please?"

Betty repeated sister Nan's suggestions to her
when she was a freshman about not making
friends too hastily. Then she arranged hours
for special lessons, helped Marie with her
schedule of classes, answered her frank queries
about the desirability of being friends with

Georgia Ames and Fluffy Dutton. Then she rushed off to settle the complicated case of Mary Jones, who lived at the other end of High Street, ate a hasty luncheon, held a lengthy conference with the Morton Hall matron, who had not the least idea how to hurry through her business, made a friendly call on " the Thorn," a student who had given some trouble the last year, and whose mother had died during the summer. And finally Betty turned up, fresh and smiling, at the Tally-ho in time to take Emily's place at the desk, while that young lady combined a marketing expedition with a drive behind Mary's new thoroughbred.

At five Fluffy and Straight appeared and ordered tea at a table drawn sociably near to Betty's desk.

" Please notice our senior dignity," observed Straight. " We're not going to be so harum-scarum any longer."

" I noticed Fluffy's senior dignity this morning," Betty told them with a twinkle.

The two exchanged significant glances and then made a simultaneous rush for Betty's desk, which they leaned over sociably, in the unmistakable attitude of those having confidential information to discuss.

"Please tell us if her name is really Montana Marie," began Straight abruptly.

"And how you happen to have her under your wing," added Fluffy.

"And then we promise to be very nice to her," concluded Straight. "Besides, Fluffy says that she likes her."

"We'll be very nice to her anyway, if you want us to, Betty," Fluffy explained sweetly. "But we're just bursting to know about her and her beautiful name."

"Just can't put our minds on anything else," murmured Straight sadly. "And I can't afford to risk a mess of warnings this year after all the trouble I had with logic when I was a junior."

"In short," concluded Fluffy impressively, "Montana Marie O'Toole is the sensation of the hour at Harding College. Do you ask me to prove it? Watch the Dutton twins forget their cakes and tea while they talk about her."

CHAPTER III

THE INITIATION OF MONTANA MARIE

MONTANA MARIE O'TOOLE was, even as Fluffy Dutton had said, the sensation of the hour at Harding College. Indeed, she bid fair to be the chief sensation of the entire year of 19—. Her cheerful interest in the curious rites and customs of college life continued undiminished, in spite of elaborate snubs from upper class girls and the crushing scorn of her fellow freshmen, who attempted, all in vain, to keep Marie (and so Marie's class) out of the public eye. Nothing escaped Montana Marie's smiling scrutiny. Her questions were frank and to the point. Her pithy comments were quoted from end to end of the Harding campus, and beyond. But her giggle was contagious, her sweetness really appealing, her appreciation of any small favors touching in its breezy Western sincerity. Montana Marie had "done" New York and the European capitals; she had been "finished" in "dear old Paree"; but she had also been born and brought up in a Montana mining camp, and she was not ashamed of that fact, nor of her very plain, as well as very peculiar, parentage. So Harding College agreed with Fluffy Dutton in liking Montana Marie. Its laugh at her was always friendly, if merciless, and in time it came to be even rather admiring. But that was not until long after the initiation of Montana Marie.

Susanna Hart planned that joyous festivity. Since Madeline Ayres had planned a similar one for Georgia and the Dutton twins and some of their Belden House classmates, and Betty Wales had explained and defended the Harding variety of initiation to an amused faculty investigating committee, there had been no official opposition to the hazing of freshmen at Harding. Hazing (Harding brand) was recognized as just an ingenious, "stunty" way of entertaining the newcomers, of finding out their best points, of helping them to show the stuff they were made of, and to take their proper places in the little college world,—in short, of getting acquainted without loss of time, or any foolish fuss and feathers.

So being initiated had speedily come to be considered an honor instead of a torment. All the most popular freshmen were initiated—in very small and select parties calculated to give each individual her due importance. And because of the extreme popularity—or prominence—of Montana Marie O'Toole, Susanna Hart decided that she should have an initiation all to herself. So she asked Marie to dinner at the Belden on a rainy Saturday night when there was nothing else going on. The initiation feature of the evening's entertainment was not mentioned to Montana Marie; it was to be sprung upon her as a pleasant little after-dinner surprise. Susanna and her sophomore and senior friends in the Belden spent the whole afternoon arranging the " mise en scène" for the mystic ceremonies ; and they made so much noise tacking up curtains and building a spring-board in Susanna's big closet that Straight Dutton, who had a bad headache and was trying to sleep it off, came up-stairs, with rage in her heart, to find out what was happening.

Fluffy, who was acting as Susanna's chief assistant, explained. " We thought you were asleep, so we didn't come to tell you," she ended.

Straight sniffed indignantly. " I was likely to be asleep—underneath this carpenter shop."

"Stay and help us, and drown your sorrows in fudge and —— "

" Noise," finished Straight crisply. " No, thanks. I'm going to ask Eugenia Ford to massage my forehead. She's wonderful at it. Tell me what everything is for, and then I'll go back."

Fluffy gleefully exhibited a glove full of wet sand which Montana Marie was to be induced to shake in the dark, as she entered the dusky Chamber of Horrors, otherwise Susanna's single. There was a part of a real skeleton to run into ; there were clammy things and hot things and wriggly things to touch ; and finally there was the spring-board to fall from, down upon a heap of pillows, surrounded by a bewildering, fluttering hedge composed of Susanna's generous wardrobe, carefully spread out on all Susanna's dress-hangers, and those of some friends.

" She'll never get out of that closet until we haul her out," concluded Fluffy joyously.

"Isn't it going to be an extra-special initiation, Straight?"

Straight nodded in silence, reëxamined all the arrangements with polite attention to details, and departed, wearing the pained expression appropriate to one with a bad headache.

Five minutes later she was sitting crosslegged on Eugenia Ford's couch, her cheeks still pale, but her eyes dancing with mirth and excitement.

"Of course I'm a loyal senior, and I ought by rights to be up-stairs with Fluffy helping the sophs," she outlined her position rapidly. "But they've got enough help without me, and the racket did bother me fearfully, and made me mad, and besides, the juniors' Rescue party that I'm going to organize will be a grand feature, so they really ought to thank me for seeming to bother them. How many juniors are there in the house, Eugenia? Well, Timmy Wentworth counts against two of the sophs, because she's so big, and that big corner double room she and Sallie Wright have is the very best place in the house for our extra-special show. Now where can we borrow masks and black dominos? I have an idea that raw oysters dipped in hot chocolate sauce would taste rather weird. They never have had uncanny eats at the initiations I've been to, so that will be an original stroke. You go tell the others and buy the oysters and borrow chocolate and find the clothes and get the night watchman to lend you a lot of rope. I'll take a nice little nap here on your couch, away from that sophomore racket, and at five we all round up in Timmy's room to arrange."

Having thus relieved herself of all minor details, after a fashion taught her by her good friend Madeline Ayres, Straight curled up among Eugenia's downy pillows, and slept sweetly and very soundly until Eugenia and Timmy Wentworth shook her awake with the information that there were not enough black dominos and it was quarter past five.

The Belden House juniors appeared at dinner that night late and rather disheveled. Straight, because she had a headache, did not appear at all, and thereby missed seeing Montana Marie sweep through the Belden House parlors between the triumphant Susanna and Fluffy Dutton, the latter not too much worried about her twin's unprecedented indisposition to miss any of the humors of the situation. For Susanna and her friends, being rather tired and hurried, and wishing also to be suitably clothed for darkling adventures in Susanna's closet, had not dressed very formally for dinner. Against their background of shirt-waists and walking skirts or plain little muslins, Montana Marie sparkled radiantly in a clinging, trailing yellow satin, cut low enough to show the lovely curves of her throat and long enough to give just a glimpse of her high-heeled gold slippers and to lend her a quite sumptuous dignity among her short-skirted companions. A jeweled fillet held her piled-up hair in the exaggerated mode of the moment—it was becoming to Montana Marie. Diamonds sparkled at her throat and on her fingers. In short, Montana Marie was perfectly dressed for twenty-two and a formal dinner,—but not for a schoolgirl nor for any little after-dinner surprise in the way of an extra-special initiation party.

"It would be tragic to have to jump off a spring-board in those clothes," Fluffy whispered sadly to a sophomore neighbor. "We'll have to manage somehow to dress her over for the part."

"She's about my size; she can take my white linen with the braided trimming," the sophomore agreed magnanimously. "It's rather dirty, I'm sorry to say, but that's really an advantage for to-night."

"I'll tell Susanna," promised Fluffy, "and she'll have to arrange. Why in the world didn't she tell Miss Montana Marie O'Toole not to dress up like a princess?"

But Susanna, though she employed all her far-famed diplomacy, could not "arrange" any changes in her guest's wonderful toilette. When she proposed a little walk in the rain, and said it would be a shame to risk spoiling that lovely dress, Montana Marie only smiled, and picked up her train.

"I shan't spoil it," she said. "I never spoil my clothes. But I'd love a walk in the rain—with you and Fluffy. Yes, or a fudge party up-stairs. Just whatever you say."

And no amount of hints and polite protests could make Montana Marie change her mind.

So it was that, still smiling and still arrayed

in clinging bejeweled yellow satin, Montana
Marie shook hands with a gloveful of wet
sand, at the door of Susanna's Chamber of
Horrors, stuck her arms through a hole in the
Curtain of Variety, and shrieked as she
grasped first a hot potato, then a large and
lively lobster, and finally a paper snake freshly
dipped in thick white paint by Fluffy, so that
it would be sure to feel extra-crawly. Next,
after she had assured her captors that she
was enjoying it all,—they inquired at intervals according to the etiquette of hazing
(Harding brand),—she was led up to the skeleton, which promptly tumbled over upon her
with a gruesome rattle of dry bones. And
finally came the spring-board and the cushions, hemmed in by Susanna's hanging dresses,
from behind which three little sophomores
delivered horrible noises, accompanying soft,
uncanny pats and pushes, while Montana
Marie, still cheerful, though badly scared,
minus one gold slipper, and quite helplessly
entangled in her long train, struggled man-
fully to regain her feet and maintain her
composure.

When they were tired of watching her try

to get out, they turned on a sudden blaze of lights, pulled down the dresses that had been hung across the door, helped Montana Marie to arise, returned her slipper, and arranged her train.

Montana Marie blinked at the lights, and smiled blandly at the assembled company. "Nothing like this in dear old Paree," she announced, gasping but happy. "Now at Miss Mallon's Select School for American Girls ——"

"Hush," commanded Fluffy. "We aren't interested in any silly little boarding-school stories. This is a grown-up college. But as you seem to want to talk, go ahead—make a speech."

"On the subject of the Fourth Dimension," put in Susanna hastily. "We are all very tired of dear old Paree."

"But I never heard of ——" began Montana Marie.

"Sh !" commanded Susanna sternly. "If you say you've never heard of a thing like the Fourth Dimension, why, here at Harding that means social ostracism. To use simpler language suitable for very verdant little girls

"GO AHEAD MAKE A SPEECH"

like you, not to have heard of the Fourth
Dimension is a mark of complete and utter
greenness, perfect and unbearable freshness,
and even worse. If you haven't heard of it,
all right, but don't say so, unless you want to
be finally and forever dropped like—like a
hot potato,"—Susanna glanced smilingly at
the Curtain of Variety,—"by the best Harding
circles. If you haven't heard of it, why, bluff.
Now don't tell me you never heard of bluffing."

" Well," began Montana Marie, still smiling
composedly, "you see I never heard of a lot
of things that you do here, because I was
mostly educated in a convent, I suppose.
President Wallace understands that. That's
why he let me in when ——"

Marie was too much absorbed in her speech,
and her audience were too busy laughing at
her confidential disclosures, to notice a slight
commotion near the door. A second later the
room was full of masked figures in black
dominos. Two especially stalwart ones
guarded the door. The rest drew a cordon
around the amazed initiators and producing
pieces of stout rope—procured, according to

Straight's directions, from the night watchman, who was under the impression that it
was wanted by the Belden House matron for
strange purposes of her own—they silently
bound their prisoners, who were too astonished
even to struggle, and started them in proces-
sion out the door and up the hall.

Suddenly a black domino cried, "Stop—I
mean—halt, prisoners! We've forgotten something."

For Montana Marie O'Toole still stood as
she had been commanded to do to make her
speech, on the quivering middle of the spring-
board in the closet, viewing the performances
of the black dominos with mingled surprise
and amusement, manifested, as usual with her,
by a smile, rather faint now, but still somehow
infectious.

"We've forgotten the principal feature," the
voice went on. "Montana Marie O'Toole, get
down. You're no longer a persecuted little
freshman. You've been nobly rescued by
your junior protectors. Now come and see
justice done on these base tormentors of youth
and beauty."

"All right," agreed Marie calmly, scrambling down from her uncertain perch and losing off a slipper again in the process.

Susanna picked it up and handed it to her meekly.

"You're a champion bluffer, if you don't know what it means," Fluffy told her admiringly. " I suppose you knew all the time that they were coming, and that was why you just giggled at everything and let us do our worst."

Montana Marie O'Toole smiled vaguely back at Fluffy. " Oh, no, I didn't know ——" she began.

" Of course she didn't know," cut in a black domino. " Do you think we ask the advice of freshmen ——"

"Straight Dutton," cried Fluffy indignantly, " what are you doing helping a lot of juniors? You belong with us."

The black domino, thus reproached, shrugged her shoulders defiantly. " You spoiled my nap and made me mad." Then she laughed. " You won't be a bit mad after we've finished with you. Truly you won't. We've got lovely stunts and the weirdest eats. Forward march, captives,—and hurry, or we shan't have time for everything."

Enthroned on Timmy Wentworth's writing table, with Eugenia Ford to coach her in the lines of her part, Montana Marie O'Toole acted as mistress of the Rescue ceremonies.

"Fluffy Dutton, turn your dress backside front and inside out and speak a piece."

" Eugenia Ford, tell us the whole and complete story of the Winsted men you have flirted with since last week Wednesday."

" Mary Mason, sing the Rosary without stopping to laugh."

" Tilly Ann Leavitt, do your Chantecler stunt—all through."

Montana Marie announced each " lovely stunt," after Eugenia had whispered it to her, with much dignity. She watched its performance gaily, and greeted its climax with a gurgle of appreciative laughter.

When the sun—it was a big jack-o'-lantern, and it had been hastily sent for from Tilly Ann's room, to make her Chantecler stunt complete—when the sun came up over Timmy Wentworth's screen and sent long, streaming rays of orange ribbon over the room and the audience, Montana Marie O'Toole lay back gasping in Eugenia's arms.

"I saw that play acted in French, in dear old Paree. Did Miss Leavitt see it there too? Did she make up that take-off herself? Oh, my, I feel so perfectly at home here now!" Montana Marie rocked back and forth in an ecstasy of mirth and satisfaction.

"The world is such a small place," she added with much originality, and smiled impartially on all classes present.

Then they turned out the lights and had the "weird eats"—the largest raw oysters to be bought in Harding, dipped in very thick, very hot chocolate sauce. And then they had "real food," namely: Cousin Kate's cookies and pineapple ice. Eugenia had requisitioned the "real food" of Betty Wales, at Straight's instigation.

"If we gallantly rescue her freshman, she certainly ought to do something nice for us," Straight had declared. "Tell her that we prefer ice to ice-cream, because we—I—have recently had a headache, and I feel for ice. Tell her she will be an angel to send the things because we haven't had a dessert that I like this whole long week."

And Betty, who understood all about campus fare, smilingly promised, and was better than her word to the extent of a huge pitcher of lemonade.

Montana Marie was proving rather an amusing protégée, she reflected that evening, after Thomas, the new door and errand boy, had been dispatched to the Belden with the " real eats." The girls liked her, in spite of her queerness, and so did the faculty ; at least several of them had spoken of her to Betty in very friendly terms. College had been open nearly a month now, but Montana Marie had not asked for any help from her official tutor except with her entrance conditions. The one in history she was almost ready to pass off, Betty thought. She made a note on her engagement pad : " Ask M. M. how freshman work is going, specially math." Betty smiled to herself, as she remembered how scared all the Chapin House crowd had been over their freshman math. And then in the end nobody had been even warned except Roberta, and that was because she was always too frightened that first year to try to recite ; Roberta was labeled a " math. shark " before she graduated.

Betty wondered how the Rescue party was

progressing. She wished she were not a "near-faculty," with faculty dignity to sustain. She longed to borrow a black domino and a mask and join the Rescue party incognito. She thought of a deliciously funny " stunt " to suggest as Susanna Hart's penalty for having instigated Montana Marie's hazing party. She hoped her freshman would be game— would make them keep on liking her—now that they had begun.

She stayed late at the Tally-ho working on her accounts, and reached the campus just in time to run into Montana Marie O'Toole being escorted home,—at top speed, owing to the exigencies of the ten o'clock rule,—by Eugenia, the Dutton twins, reunited without loss of time, and Susanna Hart.

Straight detached herself from escort duty to tell Betty all about the party. " Part two, the Rescue, was a grand, extra-special success," she explained, " and the sophs say that part one was just as good. I say, Betty, did you give us away? Did you tell Montana Marie about the Rescue ? "

Betty hadn't even seen her freshman for two days, until to-night's brief encounter.

Straight considered. "I wonder if somebody else told her. She didn't act a bit surprised. But then she never does act surprised, no matter what happens or what wild tales we stuff her with. Betty, have you noticed how you can't ever tell what she thinks?"

Betty laughed. "I never can tell what people think, Straight, unless they tell me. It's only Madeline and you clever twins who can read people's minds."

"Only some people's," Straight corrected modestly. "And I don't believe even the wonderful Madeline could read Montana Marie's. She's queer. That's the only word that describes her,—except pretty, of course,— just queer. First you laugh at her, then you like her, and before you get tired of her foolishness you get awfully interested in studying her out. And you can't. Can't make her out, I mean. Betty —— " Straight paused at the door of Morton Hall.

"Yes," laughed Betty.

"Ask her if she knew about to-night's Rescue party, will you?"

"Of course," Betty promised. "Fly now, Straight, or you'll be locked out."

" Never." Straight prepared to fly her fast-est. "I'll bet you anything, Betty Wales, that you won't ever find out. Whether she knew, I mean. Good-night, Betty."

Straight had flown.

CHAPTER IV

MONTANA MARIE TAKES A RIDE

GEORGIA AMES had missed Montana Marie's initiation party, having been engaged that evening in helping to console Mary Brooks Hinsdale for the temporary loss of her husband.

"Clever husbands are so intermittent," Mary had sighed plaintively. "Now you have them to provide tea for, and other amusements, and now they're off to the ends of the earth to deliver a lecture. And mine won't ever take me along, because my frivolous aspect rattles him when he gets up to speak. I presume," Mary smiled serenely, "that he also thinks said frivolous aspect would queer him with his learned friends; only he's too polite to put it to me so baldly. And the moral of all this, Georgia, my child, is: Don't marry a professor, unless you are prepared to take the consequences. The immediate consequence is that you've got

to be Georgia-to-the-Rescue for me this time,
and come up to spend Saturday night."

"And so," Georgia explained to Betty later,
"I wasn't on hand to be Georgia-to-the-Rescue for your freshman. But then she didn't
need me. She really didn't even need res-
cuing. And just to show her how I admire
her pluck, I've made the riding party I'm
going off with ask her to come on our Mountain Day trip."

"But she can't possibly get a horse so late
in the day," objected Betty.

"Belle Joyce has sprained her ankle and
gone home, so somebody else can have the
Imp."

Betty looked anxious. "But, Georgia dear,
you know the Imp is a pretty lively horse.
Are you sure that Marie rides well enough to
go off on him with your experienced crowd?"

"Oh, I guess so," Georgia answered easily.
"She's ridden a lot out West, she says. She's
telegraphed to Montana for her own saddle
and her riding things, and they ought to be
here to-day. When they come, I'll take her
out on a practice trip to be sure that she can
ride. Nobody wants to kill off your amusing

freshman, Betty; so don't look so awfully solemn."

Betty laughed heartily. " Well, you know I had a nice spill here once myself, and so I believe in being careful. But I think it was ever so nice of you to include Marie in your party, Georgia."

" There isn't a freshman in college who wouldn't give her best hat for the chance of going off with our crowd," Georgia declared modestly. " It's funny, isn't it, Betty, how much the girls care about getting in with the right college set?"

Betty nodded. " And I'm afraid it's not because the right college set, as you call it, generally has the most fun. It's very often only because they are silly enough to want the name of being popular."

" Snobs!" muttered Georgia scornfully. " Well, Montana Marie is no snob, and thanks mostly to you there aren't nearly so many snobs in Harding as there were when I first came up."

" Really? Do you notice a difference?" demanded Betty eagerly.

" Yes, and lots of it," declared Georgia, "so

don't work too hard this year creating the proper college spirit, because you don't need to. And don't worry about our killing off your freshman. Unless I see that she's a very good rider on our trial trip, I'll make her swap off the Imp with one of the girls who can surely manage him, and take old Polly. Old Polly wouldn't hurt a fly."

Montana Marie's pet saddle and riding clothes did not come until just in time for Mountain Day, but Georgia took her, according to promise, for the practice ride, borrowing Straight Dutton's skirt for her, and explaining that it was Harding custom not to bother about hats.

Montana Marie listened graciously to Georgia's sage advice about being very careful until you knew your horse ; and she made no objection to starting out on Polly, who was a meek-looking, gentle-gaited bay with one white foot,—the idol of timid beginners in Harding riding circles. But before they had gone a mile, Montana Marie drew rein and announced pleasantly that she couldn't ride Polly a step further.

"I suppose I must be too heavy for her.

She seems so tired, and she lags behind so. Would you be willing to change with me, Miss Ames? You are lighter, and you are used to Polly's ways. You don't blame me, do you, for hating to use up a horse?"

So Montana Marie rode Georgia's favorite Captain, who single-footed by choice but would canter if crowded to it. He cantered with Montana Marie all the way to Far-away Glen, the destination of the party. There they dismounted to drink out of a mountain spring, and Montana Marie somehow settled it that the groom from the stables should go back on Polly, Captain being restored to Georgia, and the skittish roan named Gold Heels left for herself. Georgia protested anxiously, but Montana Marie smiled and reassured her.

"Why, you can't worry about me, Miss Ames. I've ridden all my life," she said, making the roan curvet and prance on purpose. " I guess I rode before I walked. But these pancake saddles are the limit, I think. Just you wait till my own outfit comes, and then I'll show you some real riding. My, but it seems like old times to be on a horse! I had just one ride all the time we were in Paris. Riding in a park is too slow for me, and besides I hate side-saddles—you can't use anything else over there, you know—as I hate—select schools for girls," added Montana Marie in an unwonted burst of confidence.

"So you're glad to be back in America?" asked Georgia idly.

"I should say I am, Miss Ames. Some day you'll know, maybe, just how glad I am."

Georgia was too busy keeping Captain from imitating the roan's pernicious tactics in the matter of shying at dead leaves to wonder exactly what Montana Marie was driving at so earnestly.

"She will be perfectly safe on the Imp," Georgia reported later to Betty. "At least I think so, and anyhow she is perfectly set on riding him, and she said she'd never ride old Polly again, if there wasn't another horse in the world. So we shall just have to let her decide about the risks for herself. Your freshman has a mind of her own, hasn't she, Betty?"

Betty agreed laughingly. Montana Marie, when approached by her official tutor about her freshman class work, particularly freshman math., had reported easily that she guessed everything was going all right.

"But anyway, I'm planning to get my entrance conditions off first," she announced. "Then I can devote my whole time to regular work. I believe in being systematic, don't you, Miss Wales?"

Betty tried to explain that the entrance conditions were regarded by the Powers as extras, not to take the place or time of regular work. Montana Marie listened good-naturedly.

"I never could do but one thing at once, Miss Wales," she explained at last. "In Germany I forget every word I know of French, and in dear old Paree I actually almost forget my English. If I could only cut classes entirely for a week or so and get this entrance history and Latin prose off my mind!"

"Well, you can't," Betty told her decidedly. "Your having so many conditions will make all your teachers specially particular. The very least you can do, when President Wallace stretched a rule to let you in, is not to cut a single, single class, unless you are too ill to go, of course."

Montana Marie sighed plaintively. " I never was ill in my life. I think I am doing fairly well in my studies, Miss Wales. I certainly try hard enough. After all the fuss I had about getting in, I don't want to get out again yet a while. The great trouble is that there are so many social affairs all the time. When I'm looking forward to a dinner on the campus or a dance in the gym. or a walk with that cute little Miss Hart, why I just can't settle down to study. It was lucky Miss Hart had an impromptu initiation for me. I shouldn't have been able to learn a single lesson with an initiation to look forward to."

" Then if it diverts your mind to go to things, you simply mustn't go to so many, Marie." Betty tried to look severe and to speak sternly. " You must refuse some of your invitations. Or else you must learn to concentrate your mind on whatever you're doing, work as well as play. Being able to jump straight from Greek to the sophomore reception and from chemistry lab. into managing a basket-ball team is one of the most valuable things you can learn at this college. And you've got to learn it early in freshman year, or you won't ever get comfortably through your mid-years." Betty surveyed Montana Marie's unruffled calm rather despairingly.

Montana Marie smiled comfortingly back at her tutor, and then sighed faintly. "I'm not sure, Miss Wales, that I have any mind to concentrate. You see in the convent your soul was the most important thing, and in Miss Mallon's Select School for American Girls your manners and the pictures in the Louvre were the most important. But I promise you that I won't go everywhere I'm asked—not anywhere until I've passed off my history. And I promise not to cut, and I'll ask my teachers right away if my work is satisfactory."

Betty wrote her mother that night that Marie was developing wonderfully, quite as Mrs. Wales had prophesied, and that taking charge of her was really no trouble at all, because she was so anxious to carry out her part of the bargain she had made with Betty, to do her best.

"So tell Will to tell Tom Benson," Betty wrote, "that Miss O'Toole isn't a handful. I'm almost afraid she'll turn out a dig or a prig or something of that kind, she seems so anxious to do good work. But all the nicest girls like her, so I guess I needn't worry about her not having a good time."

The day before Mountain Day the history condition was removed from Miss Montana Marie O'Toole's record of scholarship, and Betty congratulated her freshman warmly and went off to spend the holiday in Babe's wonderful house on the Hudson feeling as care-free and irresponsible as if she were a freshman herself.

Georgia's riding party was to take horse—this knowing expression was also Georgia's—at the Belden at nine o'clock sharp. At a quarter before the hour Montana Marie, the only off-campus member, arrived at the rendezvous. Her habit was brown corduroy, her hat a flapping sombrero, her lovely hair was coiled in a soft knot in her neck. It looked as if it would fall down before she had mounted, but not a lock was out of place that night, when Montana Marie rode the dripping, drooping Imp into his stable-yard half an hour ahead of the others, and sweetly asked the liveryman if he would mind giving her a real horse the next time she hired one.

"Because if you can't, I guess I'll ask my father to send one of his East to me," she explained, reaching down to unbuckle her big saddle before she slipped easily out of it. " I don't mean to compare this horse with old Polly or that silly roan," she added politely. " But I do like a little real excitement when I go for a ride."

If Montana Marie had found her Mountain Day tame, the rest of the party had not lacked for " real excitement" in generous measure. Montana Marie had ridden decorously enough between Georgia and Susanna Hart out of the town and up Sugar Hill to White Birch Lane. At the turn into the woods she had produced a magenta silk bandana and knotted it coquettishly at the back of her neck.

" Now I'm a real cow-girl," she explained. " Ma can educate me all she wants, but she can't educate the West out of me. She'd never have sent me this wild and woolly outfit. She'd have written her New York tailor to come right up here and fit me out. But I like these things best, so I just telegraphed to Dad, and he did as I said. He always does. Now why don't we race up the next hill?" Montana Marie started off the Imp with a yodeling shout and a wildly waving arm that made even sedate old Polly take a keen interest in following. Susanna Hart's horse reared, and Fluffy Dutton shrieked hysterically. Then the skittish roan Gold Heels bolted down a side-path with the groom from the stable, and before he could get back to his charges' assistance, a Belden House sophomore, who was always unlucky with horses, carelessly fell off the Captain's back. True to his training the big horse stopped dead in his tracks, and Montana Marie, having seen the accident over her shoulder, rushed the Imp back, dismounted, and assisted the unlucky sophomore to her feet with the sincerest apologies for having "made any one any trouble."

"If you'd had a saddle like mine you wouldn't have fallen off," she ended regretfully. "You can't enjoy a real wild ride on those little flat seats."

"We're not out for a wild ride," Georgia rebuked her sternly. "If you want to race and make a general disturbance you must ride way ahead alone. But if I were you ——"

"Oh, I shouldn't think of stirring up anything more," declared Montana Marie demurely, pulling the Imp into a decorous park-trot beside the unlucky sophomore, who was luckily not a bit the worse for her tumble. "I'm only a little freshman, and I want to learn the college ways in riding as in other things." She secreted her magenta neckerchief again, and "rode like a perfect lady," to quote from Georgia's account of the matter, all the way to Top Notch Falls, and all the way back against the sunset, until ——

Little Eugenia Ford's horrified description of what happened next was perhaps the most vivid of those furnished to eager inquirers.

"When we were down on the meadow-road," Eugenia began that evening to an attentive audience of her house-mates, "it got a little bit dusky. We heard some horses coming fast behind us, and it was my Cousin John Ford, who is a senior at Winsted, and three men from his frat-house. They stopped to speak to me, and I introduced them to Fluffy and Montana Marie, who were riding beside me. We happened to be quite a little ahead of the others. John said something about Montana Marie's queer Mexican saddle, and that freshman put on her awful magenta handkerchief again, and asked him if he liked cow-girls and 'real exciting' rides, and of course John said yes. And she said to come on then, and hit his horse with her whip, and they just tore off in the dark." Eugenia's big brown eyes were round with horror. "John is a splendid rider or he wouldn't have stayed on, because his horse—it's one of his own and a thoroughbred—had never been touched with a whip before, and it nearly went crazy when Montana Marie whacked it. So his horse flew and the Imp flew too, and John tried to stop, but she just shouted again and again, and egged both the horses on. John telephoned me as soon as I got home, to say that his neck wasn't broken, and to inquire for hers. He seemed to think it was a joke, but for my part "— Eugenia looked as severe as so small and so pretty a young lady was able to look—" for my part I think it was unladylike and dangerous, and I hope Georgia will never want to ask her to go riding with us again. My horse almost ran too." Eugenia grew a shade more haughty. "She asked John to call and to bring his three friends. I—I'm afraid he'll come."

" I shouldn't be much surprised if he did," agreed a caustic senior, who roomed next door. " Montana Marie O'Toole is not exactly a lady, and she—well, I don't know that she is ever exactly inconsiderate except on horseback. But she's always interesting, foot or horseback. Were your crowd—were you thinking of dropping her because she mossed up your ride ? "

Eugenia flushed. " She's asked the Mountain Day party to dinner to-morrow night at the Vincent Arms. She boards there, you know. She seems to be—very rich. I don't know much about her family, but Betty Wales has met her mother and liked her. I —I do want to see the inside of that wonderful boarding-house."

" Millionairesses' Hall, isn't it called ? " asked the senior. " Yes, I've wanted to go there too, for dinner, but I don't know anybody who'll ask me. They have flowers on

the tables every night, and seven courses.
You'd better go."

Eugenia considered. "It would be fun.
Only—she was really horrid—racing off that
way with John."

"Maybe he won't call on her, after all,"
consoled the senior. "If he does—eat her
dinner first, drop her afterward. But
whether you drop her or not, she's bound to
stay in fashion here. She's interesting, lady
or no lady. Don't go riding with her, if you
don't like her Western style. But for my
part, I think she's really too good to miss.
Now isn't it just like that lucky Betty Wales
to have the most entertaining freshman, as
well as the most fascinating tea-room, to
amuse herself with?"

At the very moment when the caustic senior was making this remark, Betty Wales sat
at her desk in the fascinating tea-shop. The
entertaining freshman sat beside her. For
once she was not smiling. Spread out on the
desk before Betty were three distinct and sep-
arate warnings, in freshman math., freshman
Latin, and freshman lit., respectively. Betty
Wales had seen a few warnings before, but

she did not remember any that were quite so frank and unqualified in their condemnation of the recipient's scholastic efforts and attainments as the three euphemistically addressed to Miss M. M. O'Toole.

CHAPTER V

MADELINE AYRES had come up to Harding to celebrate the acceptance of a novel by her favorite firm of publishers. Babbie Hildreth had come too, to help Madeline celebrate, and also to talk to Mr. Thayer about that most important topic, the date of " the " wedding. And so of course the " B. C. A.'s " had appointed a special tea-drinking, to celebrate the acceptance of the novel, the visits of Madeline and Babbie, the prospect of a wedding in their midst, and the general joys involved in the state of being " Back at the College Again,"—which is what B. C. A. stood for. Equally of course the tea-drinking was to be held at the Tally-ho.

But when the hour of the grand celebration arrived, a damper was put on everything ; Betty Wales had sent a hastily scribbled note, by an accommodating freshman who was going right past the Tally-ho, to say that she was too busy to come.

"She's losing her sporting spirit," declared Madeline sadly. "In days gone by you could depend on Betty's turning up for any old lark. She might be late, if she happened to be pretty busy, but she always got there in the end."

"And I wanted to ask her about wedding dates," wailed Babbie plaintively. "I can't have my wedding when Betty can't come. She's almost as important as the groom."

"Betty is awfully important to such a lot of people," complained Mary Brooks Hinsdale, who was looking particularly fascinating in her new fall suit, the christening of which had added an extra spice of interest to the grand tea-drinking. "She is altogether too capable for her own good. If she were only as lazy, or as unreliable, or as devoid of ideas and energy, as most of those here present, she wouldn't find it so hard to escape for tea-drinkings and other pleasant festivities. Which one of her dependents has her in its clutches this afternoon, I wonder?"

Babbie, to whom Betty's note had been addressed, consulted it for further details. "She says she's got to tutor a freshman," Babbie explained after a minute. " I suppose she is helping along some one who can't afford to pay for regular lessons. Seems to me there ought to be girls enough in college to do that sort of thing without putting it off on Betty. Betty is too valuable to be wasted on mere tutoring."

" Poor girls ought not to need to be tutored," announced Madeline, in her oracular manner. "Unless they are bright and shining lights in their studies, they ought not to try to go through college at all."

" But Madeline ——" chorused the permanent B. C. A.'s—the ones who were always on hand in Harding, because they were either faculty or faculty wives. " But Babbie—you two don't understand. Haven't you ·heard about Betty's freshman?"

" No, we haven't," chorused the new arrivals. " Tell us this minute."

Mary finally got the floor. " My children," she began in her most patronizing style, " our precious Betty Wales is not engaged in assisting some needy under classman along the royal road to learning, as you seem to suppose. She is acting as special tutor to the only daughter of a Montana mining magnate. Named Montana Marie after the mine, pretty as a picture, clever at horseback riding but not at mathematics,—and the grand sensation of Harding College just at present," ended Mary proudly. Then the permanents told the "properly excited" newcomers the whole story of Montana Marie O'Toole.

"She sounds extremely interesting," said Madeline reflectively, when they had finished.

"Almost like a ready-made heroine," suggested Mary, winking knowingly at the others.

Madeline nodded absently, and everybody laughed at what Mary called the egotism of the literary instinct.

"Why, haven't you ever caught Madeline squinting at you to see if you'll do for a book?" demanded Mary, elaborating her point. "She relates everything, even friends, to her Literary Career. I wore my new suit to-day in the frantic hope that she'd like my looks well enough to put me into a play. I should simply adore seeing myself in a play," sighed Mary.

" Well, you never will," Madeline assured her blandly. "Not while you call me 'my child,' and patronize me instead of my tea-shop."

Mary listened, wearing her beamish smile. " Egotism of the literary instinct again—she makes a personal matter out of everything. Now, if you've quite finished explaining your methods of literary work, suppose we return to the business of the meeting, which is —— "

" Which seems to be your frivolous methods of securing the attention of the wise and great by wearing new clothes," cut in Madeline promptly. " A very interesting subject, too, isn't it, my children ? "

Mary faced the challenger coldly. " The real business of the meeting," she announced, " is the rescue of Betty Wales from the clutches of her too-numerous jobs, charities, helpful ideas, and noble ambitions, including that interesting but heavily conditioned fresh-man, Montana Marie O'Toole."

" But I thought Georgia had been regularly 'elected' to look out for Betty," suggested Christy Mason.

" Well, Georgia is only one," explained

Helen Chase Adams seriously, "and being a prominent senior keeps her fairly busy, I imagine. And then Betty doesn't want to be rescued. It's very hard to look out for a person that doesn't want you to look out for him—her," amended Helen hastily, with a vivid blush that instantly created another digression among the B. C. A.'s.

"I thought you didn't like men, Helen Chase."

"Who is he? Who is your protégé who objects to being looked after, Helen?"

"When you said 'him' you were only trying to speak good English? Well, isn't 'her' as good English as 'him'?"

"You might as well own up to him right off and save yourself a lot of trouble. Detective Ayres will shadow you till you confess."

But Helen displayed a hitherto unsuspected talent for clever sparring. "It's just like you girls to make a lot out of a little," she declared, so earnestly that everybody saw she meant it. "That's why we have such good times,—because you make all the stupid little things in life seem interesting."

"Well, don't dare to deny that you're a

stupid little thing," Mary told her, with an appreciative pat to emphasize that she was only joking. " And please be duly thankful that we can make even you seem interesting."

" Oh, I am grateful," Helen told her, with pretty seriousness. " But you ought to keep within the probabilities, and you ought to have more variety about your inventions. We've got romances enough on hand, without making up one for me."

" The business of this meeting ——" began Mary again at last, pounding hard on the table with one of the fascinating fat mustard jars which Madeline had summarily bought in London to start the Tally-ho Tea-Shop. " The business of this meeting ——"

" Is just coming in at the door," Rachel Morrison laughingly finished Mary's sentence for her.

And sure enough, Betty Wales, looking very young, very pretty, also very care-free and happy for a person in dire need of rescue, was shutting the door with one hand, giving Emily Davis a handful of letters and memoranda with the other, and telling Nora about a special dinner order for that evening as she slipped off her ulster. Then she made a bee-line for Jack o' Hearts' stall and the Merry Hearts.

"Let me in—way in, please," she begged, scrambling past Babbie, Helen, and Mary to the most secluded seat at the back of the stall. "I came after all, because I wanted some fun, and I won't be dragged out to talk to anybody about dinners they want me to plan, or Student's Aid things, or Morton Hall things—or even a conditioned freshman," she concluded with a particularly vindictive emphasis on the last phrase.

"Hear! Hear!" cried Christy Mason.

"Oh, now I think maybe she'll run away again to come to my wedding," sighed Babbie, in deep relief.

"After all, she hasn't lost her sporting spirit," Madeline rejoiced. "She's the same old Betty Wales, better late than never, and quite capable of looking out for herself, as well as for all the bothering jobs and charities and incompetent friends and touchy millionaires and insistent suitors and helpful ideas and noble ambitions that clutch at her with octopus fingers and threaten to drag her down."

"Don't talk like a book, Madeline," Mary criticized. "And don't be too cock-sure that you're right. Just because Betty couldn't stand it another minute and has rushed to cover, so to speak, in our midst, I for one refuse to be convinced that she doesn't need help in fighting the octopus."

Betty brushed a rebellious curl out of her eyes with a tired little gesture, and stared curiously at the disputants. "What in the world are you talking about?" she demanded. "Mary dear, please explain, because Madeline's explanations usually just mix things up more than ever."

Mary explained, noisily assisted by all the other B. C. A.'s, including Madeline, who "explained" at length how forgiving she was by nature, advised Mary to adopt the proud peacock as her sacred bird, and finally demanded of Betty if she—Madeline—hadn't been perfectly correct in saying that she— Betty—was perfectly capable of getting along all right, if only she was not hampered by one more bother,—the unasked advice and assistance of the B. C. A.'s.

"Of course you're right, Madeline," Betty

assured her, stirring her tea absently and forgetting to eat any of her muffin. "I detest people who can't get along alone. It's silly to try to do a lot more than you can, and then expect somebody to come along and take it off your hands. I hope I'm not that kind." Betty dropped her spoon with a clatter, and, sitting up very straight, faced the table with a tragic look in her eyes and a desperate, determined set to her soft red lips.

"Girls," she began, with a sudden change of tone that matched her changed expression, "can you remember solid geometry? I can't. I never did know anything about Latin prose, so there's no reason why I should now. But not knowing the geometry worries me. I think it's getting on my nerves. And then," she went on, as the little circle only stared at her in curious silence, " Marie's lit. notes are just a mess. Mine were too, and anyhow I've lost my note-book. Is yours here, Helen? Could I take it, and Christy's? I'm sure I could manage if I had a decent note-book or two."

"Speaking of clear and lucid explanations ——" began Madeline slowly. Then she reached across the table to hug Betty comfortingly. "You shall have all the decent notebooks in 19—, if you want them, you poor thing. And I'm truly sorry that mine isn't one of them. As for solid geometry, I'll wager that not a person in this crowd could demonstrate—is that the right word for it?—a single proposition. And as for Latin prose, it's a gift from the gods. You can't learn it. Even Professor Owen, who is a genius, can't teach it. So stop worrying here and now, and eat that muffin before somebody is tempted beyond what she can bear, and a theft is committed in our midst."

"Is all this trouble caused by Montana Marie O'Toole?" inquired Christy practically.

Betty nodded, being too busy with the muffin to speak.

"Then," Mary announced with decision, "what she needs is three regular graduate tutors, who specialize in lit., math., and Latin prose, and who will come to her rescue at any hour or hours of the day or night, at about one-fifty per."

Betty swallowed a mouthful hastily, to say, "They wouldn't help her any, Mary. They'd give up in despair after about one lesson. She's not stupid exactly, but she's poorly prepared, and her mind is—well, queer. Besides, I promised President Wallace. I agreed to 'undertake' her, as Mrs. O'Toole calls it, before he agreed to let her enter with so many conditions. She's going to be positively broken-hearted if she fails at mid-years, and I think "—Betty hesitated—" I don't think President Wallace will ever have any use for me again if she does. And I am busy with other things, and I never did know Latin prose, and—I'm about in despair." Betty paused abruptly and attacked the remains of the muffin as if the eating of it would work a magic cure of all her woes.

" Betty," asked Rachel after a minute, " does this freshman try? Does she want to get through enough to work for it?"

" She doesn't know how to really work, Rachel, but she tries as hard as she can. She is awfully sweet and awfully sorry about making extra trouble. And of course you all understand," Betty blushed a little, " that I'm being paid—altogether too much, I thought when they offered it—for looking after her."

Betty laughed suddenly. "Did you hear about her Mountain Day exploit? I had to speak to her about that, of course, to tell her that she mustn't wear a magenta handkerchief, and shout so loud on the public highway, and otherwise make herself too conspicuous. And instead of being huffy, she thanked me and sent me violets. Oh, she's a dear! She's worth a lot of trouble, only I'm not bright enough to tutor her, and the regular ones would be sure to get provoked or discouraged at her queer ways, and just consider her hopeless, and let her drift along, and finally be flunked out at mid-years."

"She ought to be flunked out, oughtn't she?" inquired Helen Adams acutely. "I mean, she probably can't ever keep her work up to the required standard without a lot of help."

Betty admitted sadly that she never could. "But she needs the life here, Helen, almost more than any girl who ever came to Harding. And if I can help her to have a year or two of it, I shall,—as long as she keeps on trying to do her part."

"Oh, yes, of course," agreed Helen uncertainly.

"Is she in your freshman division, Helen?" demanded Mary Brooks, after a whispered conference with Babbie. "I judged not. Very well then. You are hereby elected to coach her in lit. No rule against a faculty's doing a little friendly tutoring, is there? My husband hasn't condescended to bother with any since he got to be head of his department, but before that —— " Mary finished the explanation with a wave of her hand. "In the theme work that goes with lit., Madeline is hereby elected to come to the front. Madeline, I presume you forgot, when you were talking about solid geometry, that our clever little Christy here has given up her faculty job to take a Ph. D. in math. She is hereby elected to assist Miss O'Toole to the comprehension of sines and co-sines, and so forth—or do sines and co-sines belong to trig.? And for Latin prose," Mary's beamish smile broke out radiantly, "of course you don't know it, because it happened before your day, but Latin prose happens to be the one useful thing I ever learned. I say useful, because after all these years, I can use my one small scholarly accomplishment. Oh, I've kept it up! George

Garrison Hinsdale has seen to that. Whenever he seems to be getting a bit tired of my frivolous appearance and conversation, I read him a little out of Horace or Juvenal or Cicero's letters, and he's so proud of me that I wish I had more scholarly accomplishments. Only,"—Mary smiled serenely,—" he says he likes me just as I am. And so, being the Perfect Wife, I will now turn into the Perfect Tutor, and get Marie Montana O'Toole through her Latin prose."

" The business of this meeting having been disposed of," Madeline took up the tale, " I hereby demand that we begin to celebrate in honor of me and my forthcoming novel."

" And to discuss wedding dates," added Babbie, " in honor of me and my Young-Man-Over-the-Fence."

" Don't you think," suggested Rachel, " that first we'd better let Betty, who has just said she prefers to manage her own affairs, say what she wants to do about Mary's elections ? "

" When you are elected ——" began Mary, but Helen, Rachel, and Christy, the serious members, silenced her.

" Now, Betty," ordered Rachel. Betty

looked solemnly from Helen to Christy, from Christy to Madeline, and finally at Mary.

" Would you really do it, girls?" she asked at last.

" Of course," said Helen quietly.

" You can count on me, if you want me," Christy told her.

" I can't promise till I've looked over the freshman," Madeline qualified. " If she is anywhere near as interesting as she sounds, I'll 'undertake' her theme-work with much pleasure."

" I'm simply dying to display my one accomplishment," Mary declared feelingly.

Betty gave a long, happy sigh. " Then of course I want you all to help," she said. " I was just about in despair when I came rushing down here. And now—you're not regular tutors. You understand things. You know how I feel—and how Prexy feels. I couldn't explain to a regular tutor that for some unknown reason Prexy cares a lot about Marie's passing her exams. And I couldn't tell them why she herself needs so much to stay on here. But you'll see it all. Oh, dear! I'm so happy!" Betty crunched one of Cousin

Kate's cookies, and smiled radiantly at Mary, who had " elected " everything so beautifully.

" Well," inquired Babbie, after a polite interval, " now can we begin to celebrate and plan weddings ? "

" Easily," Mary Brooks assured her. " Only don't forget, all of you, whether you have been elected tutors yet or whether you haven't, that you've each and all got to help. The B. C. A.'s have adopted a new object—we have undertaken Montana Marie O'Toole—and it may need our entire combined effort to make her a credit to us and to Harding. But we've got to do it. And do it we will ! "

" Hear ! Hear ! " from Madeline.

" The B. C. A.'s to the Rescue ! " cried Helen.

" Betty Wales and her freshman ! " added Christy.

They drank the toasts with much enthusiasm in fresh cups of tea—poured out without the use of a strainer, because the next " feature " on the program was to be tea-ground fortunes all around, read by that past-mistress of the fine art of making everything interesting, Miss Madeline Ayres.

CHAPTER VI

THE INTERVENTION OF JIM

MONTANA MARIE O'TOOLE accepted with her accustomed submissive sweetness the new tutors "elected" to office by Mary Brooks Hinsdale and tactfully introduced to their victim by Betty Wales, who explained just why she had consented to a division of labor.

"They do seem to make me understand better," Marie told Betty, a few days after the beginning of the new régime. "That Miss Mason is awfully smart, isn't she? But fortunately she isn't anything like that smart tutor I had last summer. Miss Mason makes me puzzle things out for myself. It takes a lot of her valuable time, I'm afraid." Poor Marie sighed deeply. "It's a great responsibility, wasting the time of a faculty and a—what's that Miss Mason is?—oh, yes, a Fellow in Mathematics. And I can't pay Miss Adams, because it is against the rules for the faculty to be paid for tutoring. Is it against the rules for me to send her flowers every day, Miss Wales?"

Betty remembered how violets used to make Helen's eyes shine, and said no. "Only you mustn't be extravagant, you know. Every day is much too often to send flowers."

"I can't say that I think it's any too often to get flowers," smiled Montana Marie. "And so far Pa hasn't objected to any of my bills. It's fortunate, isn't it, that my father isn't as poor as I am stupid?"

"You're not stupid," Betty encouraged her. "If you'll only keep on trying ——"

"Oh, I shall keep trying." Montana Marie was firm as a rock on that point. "I've inherited my father's stick-to-itiveness, if I haven't inherited his brains. Now I might have been a flyaway like Ma. And in that case things would have been pretty hopeless, wouldn't they, Miss Wales?"

Two days later Montana Marie appeared at Betty's office, the fire of determination in her lovely eyes.

"I saw a sign on the bulletin-board that said there was an unexpected vacancy in Morton Hall. Is that so?"

Betty nodded abstractedly, her finger on the place where she had left off reading a letter from Mr. Morton.

"Then I want to fill it. I've got to leave the Vincent Arms because it's too diverting to my mind. If I could live in the dormitory with you, I should be made!"

"But Morton Hall is a special dormitory," Betty explained patiently, as she had many times before, to admirers who had thought it would be the making of them to live in "her dormitory." "And you're not eligible." She went into details. "So you can't possibly come, and if you could I don't think you'd like it. The harder a person works the more she needs recreation. But most of my girls have had too much work and too little play all their lives long. They don't know how to play the way Georgia Ames and Miss Hart and the Duttons do. You'd find them dull after the others."

"Then in that case my mind would stay right on my work. I'm just the opposite from them, Miss Wales. I've had too much play and too little work all my life until now. They say opposites attract, so I'm sure

I should get along splendidly with those girls."

"But you're not eligible," Betty repeated.

Montana Marie considered that. "Suppose no poor girl wants to come in just at present," she suggested at last. "Moving in the middle of the term is a bother, isn't it? Don't most girls promise to keep their rooms right through the term or even for the whole year? Couldn't I have the room as long as it is empty,— just until some eligible girl wants it?"

Montana Marie didn't mind moving in, with the strong probability of having to move out again very soon; she had lived in trunks and hotels most of her life, and was used to picking up at a moment's notice whenever her flyaway mother got tired of eating Swiss honey, or buying Dutch silver, or studying German art, and decided to move on.

The vacant room that Betty had advertised on the bulletin-board was a third floor single, but when the Thorn, who shared one of Morton Hall's few doubles, begged quite pathetically for a chance to room alone, Betty had not the heart to refuse her. Secretly, too, she was relieved at the prospect of thus finally settling

the question of Montana Marie's coming into
the house; for in spite of her protégée's ex-
cellent logic, Betty doubted the wisdom of
mixing such alien elements as Montana Marie
and the Morton Hall girls, and if anybody
suffered from the situation she felt sure it
would not be the exuberant Montana Marie,
with a mind of her own and a genius for getting what she wanted. Still Marie had been
thoroughly in earnest in wanting to find a
boarding place where she could study without
interruption. Betty broke the news to her
gently.

" Matilda Thorn's—I mean Matilda Jones's
roommate," she explained, " is a funny little
junior from Corey Corners, New Hampshire.
She taught a district school for two years, to
earn money enough to justify her in beginning
her college course. In the summers she is
waitress in one of the big White Mountain
hotels, not far from where she lives, and she
usually earns a little extra by taking care of
some rich woman's children when their nurse
wants a holiday or an evening off."

Montana Marie listened intently. " She
must know how to concentrate her mind, if

she does all that. I should think she'd be an
ideal roommate for me, shouldn't you, Miss
Wales? But maybe she won't like me.
Could you arrange to have us meet, Miss
Wales, and then you could ask her to say
honestly what she thought, and if she didn't
object to me I could move in right away."

Montana Marie's calm determination to look
on the bright side of things took the wind out
of Betty's opposition, just as, a little later, her
radiant, magnetic charm won from the rather
washed-out, nervous junior from Corey Corners an eager assent to Betty's proposal.
Montana Marie, five trunks, a Mexican saddle
and a striped Parisian hat-box containing a
hat that was too big for any compartment in
the pigskin hat-trunk, appeared without loss
of time at Morton Hall. Being systematic,
Montana Marie immediately set to work at
disposing of her possessions within the limited
area of half a rather small room and half a
very small closet. After an hour's work and
ten minutes' thoughtful contemplation, she invited her new roommate, who was trying to
write an argument paper, to go down-town
and help find a carpenter. The roommate

compromised by telling Marie where the best carpenter in Harding was to be found, and Marie went off happily. A minute later she reappeared with a question.

"I'm going to have him make me a box to go under my bed. Do you keep things under your bed? You don't? Then do you mind if I have him make two boxes? I have such a silly lot of clothes. Oh, thank you so much. You're the nicest roommate! Sure there are no errands I can do for you?"

Without looking up from her work, the strenuous little junior said no to that, for at least the third time; but when Marie presented her with a box of chocolates, evidently as a reward for being obliging about the bed-box, she relaxed her Spartan discipline and ate so much candy that she had indigestion, and was compelled to finish her argument paper in a style far inferior to that in which she had begun it. This adventure made her wary, and however easily the rest of Morton Hall fell into Montana Marie's enticing snares, her roommate kept aloof. Her name was Cordelia Payson, but Montana Marie always referred to her by Fluffy Dutton's title, "The Concentrating Influence," which Straight Dutton shortened, for her own and others' convenience, to " Connie."

The carpenter recommended by " Connie " duly produced two bed-boxes, after Montana Marie's design, which included castors, brass handles for pulling them out and lifting the covers, and interior upholstery of pale blue satin, violet-scented. When they were delivered, Montana Marie again attacked the problem of emptying the five trunks which had effectively blocked the hallway since her arrival. When she had done her best with the bed-boxes, there was still a trunkful of dresses to dispose of. Montana Marie again spent ten minutes in contemplation, and then sallied forth to order a closet pole arranged on a pulley, and equipped with two dozen dress-hangers.

" I'll keep it up in that waste space under the ceiling," she explained to the Concentrating Influence. " I'll hang my evening dresses on it, and things I don't like and seldom wear. When I want to let it down, it won't kill me to empty out part of the closet on to some chairs. Otherwise,"—Montana Marie surveyed the tightly wedged mass of clothes cheerfully,—"otherwise I'm afraid it wouldn't plough through that mass and drop down. I've got too many things, that's evident. When mid-years are over and I have a little time to turn around in, I'll sort them out and get rid of all but what I strictly need. And then," she giggled cheerfully, "it will be time to get a lot of new clothes for spring. I love spring clothes, don't you?"

"I've got to finish reading this book to-night," the Concentrating Influence told her primly, planting her elbows on her desk, and stuffing her fingers into her ears.

"Oh, excuse me," begged Montana Marie contritely. "I'm a dreadful bother. I talk too much. When you finish the book, could you show me a little about these originals that come after the twenty-sixth proposition?"

The Concentrating Influence had not forgotten her solid geometry. With casual assistance from her, and the definite and determined help of Mary Brooks Hinsdale and her corps of selected tutors, Montana Marie was making some slight progress. Betty's part was to keep Marie fully impressed with the slightness of the progress and the need for keeping up all of her work instead of letting part slide while she devoted herself to the mastery of one particularly troublesome subject; also to preach her tactful little sermons about the rights of roommates who were too obliging to object to being imposed upon. After one of these lectures Montana Marie always presented the Concentrating Influence with candy or flowers in absurdly generous quantities.

But it was not the candy and flowers that made the junior from Corey Corners feel as if, after having "scraped along" for years, she had suddenly begun to live. It was Montana Marie's unconscious assumption that she, Cordelia Payson, was a wonderful person, that all Harding College thought so, that girls like Georgia Ames and the Duttons and even that snobbish Eugenia Ford had noticed how well she did in argument, had been sorry she didn't "make" the class hockey team, and had wished they knew her better.

Montana Marie could not help saying pleasant things; she had been educated to do so. She could not help admiring mental concentration; Betty Wales had talked nothing else

to her all the year and " Connie " illustrated all
Betty's points as perfectly as if she had been
created for no other purpose.

So it was small credit to Montana Marie that
she made Cordelia Payson happy. Neither
was it at all to her credit that she was instru-
mental in bringing Jim Watson hot-foot to
Harding to investigate the supposedly prevail-
ing dissatisfaction with Morton Hall, and incidentally to give the overworked Betty Wales
two splendid, all-the-afternoon rides, and, in
addition, the restful feeling that she was being
looked after by a resourceful and a resolute
young man.

It all came about in this way. One day
when Marie had finished a Latin lesson with
Mrs. Hinsdale, that lady walked back to
the campus with her pupil on the way to a
reception in town. Mary inquired solicitously
for Betty, whom she had not seen for several
days.

"She's all right, I guess," explained Marie
easily. "Only she's sort of absent-minded,
and I notice that she doesn't eat much."

"She's overdoing dreadfully," sighed Mary.

Montana Marie considered. " As far as I

have noticed I should say that a person feels better for working hard. Ma does nothing, and Pa never takes a vacation, and he's a lot stronger than Ma is, and happier. But work is one thing, and worry is another," sighed Marie. " Worrying uses a person up like anything. Maybe Miss Wales has something on her mind. Who is this Mr. Jim Watson that you all tease her about, Mrs. Hinsdale?"

Mary explained, with a dignity that was quite lost on Montana Marie, about Jim and Eleanor, Jim and Morton Hall, and Jim and Betty.

" Wonder if she'd like to see him," speculated Marie. " She seemed awfully cheerful when I saw her in the summer, right after he'd been in Cleveland. For my part I should certainly like to see him." Marie sighed again. " I get so sick of having no men to talk to—not even faculty men. Every single one of my divisions recites to a woman."

That night Montana Marie let her mind wander shamefully from math., lit., and Latin prose. At last her contemplative smile flashed out into sudden, mischievous brilliancy. Selecting a sheet of her best lavender-tinted, violet-scented note-paper, she covered it rapidly with her sprawling, unformed characters, and directed it to Mr. James Watson, in care of his firm, the name of which she had fortunately remembered from Mary's recital.

Two days later Jim Watson, grinning sheepishly, stuck his head, in his accustomed furtive fashion, in at Betty's office door. Finding only one small person, with curls and a dimple, in the office, Jim came in a little further, and stood awaiting developments, grinning now much more cheerfully.

"What in the world are you doing here?" demanded Betty breathlessly, jumping up to shake hands.

Jim strolled over to the desk. "Don't get up." He sat down solemnly in the visitors' chair. "Don't you really know why I'm here?"

"No-o," gasped Betty, dreadfully afraid of what might be coming next. "But I know something else. You ought to be hard at work in New York."

"I have come," Jim began very solemnly,

"to investigate serious charges brought against the efficiency of the architects, particularly the resident architect-in-charge, of Morton Hall. My first duty is naturally to ascertain whether you are personally convinced of the truth of said charges. We aim to please."
Jim grinned again. "Particularly, to please one small secretary, with curls and a dimple, and a lot too much to do."

Betty leaned back in her big chair and wrinkled her face into a delightful, childlike, all-over smile. "Please explain, Jim. It's mean to tease a person like me that can't ever see through it."

Jim frowned, a portentous, businesslike frown. "Haven't I made myself clear, Miss Secretary?" He fumbled in his pockets, and produced with a flourish Montana Marie's lavender-tinted, violet-scented, scrawling note. "I got this communication yesterday, and I came right up to see about it." He handed the note to Betty.

" *Mr. James Watson,*
"Dear Sir : .
"You didn't do a very good job on Morton Hall. There is a lot of waste space

under the ceilings of the closets. They are
also too small. So are the double rooms.
The halls are too narrow when there are trunks
around. I have fixed my closet. I think it
would help you in your work to see how I
did it.

"Miss Wales, whom I believe you know,
acts rather tired these days.

"Yours respectfully,
"MARIE O'TOOLE,
"A Morton Hallite."

Betty puzzled out Marie's hieroglyphics
slowly, read the note through again, and
sighed despairingly, "What will that girl do
next?" Then she laughed till the tears
came. Then she turned severely upon Jim.

"You could see that it was all nonsense.
Why in the world did you bother to come
rushing up here on account of a piece of foolishness like that?"

Jim only grinned. "I wanted to meet
Miss Marie O'Toole of Morton Hall," he announced calmly. "Have you any objections?" Then he went on, in a different tone,
"I say, Betty, be a good fellow, and let's go
riding after lunch. I'm feeling a bit stale,—
honestly I am. An office-man like me ought

"I'VE PASSED OFF MY ENTRANCE LATIN"

never to have been brought up on ranches. If I hadn't acquired the fresh-air-and-exercise habit when I was a kid, I might be able to make a reputation now. But I can't stick to a desk long enough."

"Miss O'Toole will ride with you, poor tired man," laughed Betty. "She comes from the West, too, and she rides like an Amazon, so she'll give you all the exercise you want, trying to keep up with her."

"Thanks," said Jim briefly. "I prefer you. Say yes, Betty, like a lady, and I'll clear right out and let you do a morning's work in peace."

Betty hesitated and was lost.

"At two then," Jim sang back gaily as he "cleared out."

Five minutes later Montana Marie appeared in Betty's office looking particularly radiant. "I just stopped in to tell you that I've passed off my entrance Latin," she said. "I knew you'd be glad——" Her eyes fell on the lavender-tinted note, which Jim had forgotten to recover, and she flushed guiltily.

"You shouldn't have done such a thing," Betty told her severely, as her glance followed

Marie's. "Mr. Watson has just been here. He thought—he wanted——" Betty stopped short, and her merry laughter rang out so loud that the psychology class, which was reciting next door, heard it and wondered.

"Mr. Watson will be at the Morton for dinner to-night," Betty began again, smiling this time, "so be sure not to go out anywhere, because I shall need you to help entertain him."

"I guess you don't need me," beamed Montana Marie. "I rather guess not! But I'll be there. You can count on that, Miss Wales. I—I'm sorry if I've bothered you, but——" Marie stopped and slipped softly out, for Betty was not listening. With a shining, far-away look in her eyes, and a smile on her lips, she was thinking of—something else.

"I'm not sorry,—not a bit sorry," murmured Montana Marie, hurrying off to her next class. She did not refer to the fact that, by delaying too long in Betty's office, she had made herself late again—the second time that week—for freshman math.

CHAPTER VII

"BINKS" AMES, otherwise Elizabeth B. Browning Ames and first cousin to Georgia, was now a sophomore. Being a strenuous little person and addicted to walks in all weather, she had grown even thinner and browner than she had been as a freshman. When she timidly discovered a friend in a crowd of girls she did not know and flashed her a friendly greeting, Binks seemed to be all wonderful big gray eyes and wonderful sweet sympathy.

"Binks is peculiar," Georgia explained her tersely. "Couldn't help that, could she, with a mother who goes in for Browning and Municipal Improvement and Suffrage and the Uplifting of the Drama and all such nonsense? Binks is lovely to her—pretends to take an interest in all her isms, and bluffs about understanding Robert Browning and Henry James, and about liking her name. But it's all bluff. Binks is just as sensible as I am, and lots and lots more—decent," ended the unsentimental Georgia. "Takes home stray cats, you know, and goes walking with freaks, —and doesn't mind the bother. I never in all my life set eyes on as many stray cats as Binks finds homes for in a good average week. Of course Esther Bond is her big discovery. She was responsible for getting Esther into the Morton, you know, and since then Esther has mysteriously developed into the biggest all-around Senior Star that we've got."

"Really?" asked Straight. "That queer Miss Bond?"

Georgia nodded solemnly. "Jumped into things like that." She flashed out a capable hand. "Argus board, Senior Play Committee, and I guess Ivy Orator. Of course Helena Mason's dropping out gave Esther an extra-good chance to step in, but it's wonderful all the same. It must be lots of fun to be a perfectly Dark Horse like her. People would be so agreeably surprised that they'd appreciate you even more than you deserve."

"Instead of wondering how in the world a commonplace girl like Georgia Ames ever got to be so popular," mimicked Fluffy, the tease.

"I say, Georgia," demanded Straight, who liked college because it offered her the chance of knowing such a variety of people, and so of satisfying every mood, and developing every trait of her own complex character. "If you've got a cousin as clever as all that, why don't you let us meet her? I don't believe I ever so much as heard of her before. We ought to be looking up the eligible sophs, you know. Dramatic Club's first sophomore election isn't so very far off. Is Elizabeth B. B. Ames a possibility?"

Georgia gave a little start of surprise. "Why, I don't know. Honestly I never thought of her as one, and yet compared to some girls that are being rushed and discussed, and to some that are expecting it—you see, Binks is—well, different. I can't imagine her in Dramatic Club. She's so queer that she might actually refuse to come in."

"You said she was just as sensible as you are, Georgia," Fluffy reminded her. "That's not so much—but at least you didn't refuse Dramatic Club."

"Have a tea-drinking and let us see her," Straight settled the controversy briskly. "I for one want to see her. Come along now or we shall be late for the hockey."

A few days later Georgia, finding a free half-hour on her hands, went over to the Westcott House to see Binks. Not having paid much attention to the college career of her peculiar cousin from Boston, Georgia was surprised and pleased to find said cousin's room full of a departing House Play Committee, who were loud in their praises of Binks's ability.

"It's only that I sew costumes for them," Binks explained when they had gone, leaving the room still fairly full of gilt crowns, ermine robes, and foresters' doublets and hose of Lincoln green. "I love to sew, only I don't know how very well."

Georgia surveyed her cousin critically. "Should you like to belong to Dramatic Club?" she asked abruptly.

Binks smoothed out a bit of purple canton flannel that looked exactly like velvet with loving little pats. "I don't know. Do you belong? Is it fun?"

"I belong," Georgia told her, "and I think it's fun, but I suppose some people might not—if they were queer enough in their tastes."

"It's nothing like any of Mother's clubs, is it?" inquired Binks anxiously. "I don't care about that kind of fun—writing papers, and speaking to the legislature about changing laws, and all that."

"Binks Ames," began Georgia solemnly, "don't you honestly know more than you're pretending to about Dramatic Club? Because if you don't you ought to join for your own good and to learn a little something about college life."

Binks smiled vaguely. "I don't seem to have time to do all the things you do, Georgia. You see, I have to specialize in economics to please Mother, and in history to please Father, and in astronomy to please myself. And then there are so many queer girls that I get mixed up with, as I did with Esther Bond and Miss Ellison—the poetess person. She is forever taking me for walks and spouting poems to me all the way. I tell her that I don't know anything about poetry, but either she doesn't believe me or she can't find any one else who will listen."

"No reason why she should bother you," grumbled Georgia, who began to think that Binks might be worth cultivating.

"Oh, yes it is," Binks told her seriously. "You see, she believes in her poetry, and I guess it is all right enough. Anyway, if she stopped believing in it, she would be too discouraged to go on trying to write it. So if I can keep her going until she's sure one way or the other, why, it's little enough for a general utility person like me to do."

Georgia sniffed. "I hope some of the numerous geniuses that have sponged on you will amount to something,—and that some of the cats you have picked up will take prizes at Cat Shows."

"But I don't pick them up because they are nice cats," objected Binks solemnly, "only because they are lost, poor things!"

"Don't forget about having tea with us to-morrow," said Georgia, getting ready to leave. Her half-hour was up, and besides, she hated queer theories.

Binks did not forget to come for tea with

Georgia and Georgia's friends. She arrived on time, and becomingly dressed. She listened with gratifying appreciation to the sprightly conversation kept up by Fluffy and Susanna Hart, with some help from the others. She talked enough to be agreeable, and not enough to seem overanxious to make a favorable impression on the leading spirits of Dramatic Club, who could " make " her career at Harding, if they thought it worth while to include her in the enchanted company of the sophomores who " went in " at the first sophomore election.

As a matter of fact Binks did not know that the tea-drinkers all belonged to Dramatic Club. She did not guess why she had been asked to the tea-drinking. She had indeed entirely forgotten Dramatic Club, and had never given a second thought to Georgia's question about her wanting to be elected to it.

Georgia, being a close observer, saw all this, and made up her mind to work hard for Binks's election. Her little cousin's extreme unworldliness made her seem to the straightforward, clear-headed Georgia a rather pathetic object, to be looked out for and defended, and secured the rights and privileges that she herself did not know enough to demand. And, as what Georgia said always " went " with her large and very influential circle of friends, Binks was promptly slated as one of the fortunate sophomores whom Dramatic Club was to single out as those most wanted in its councils.

While this was being decided casually on the way up the Belden House stairs, Binks was sitting alone in her little room, staring out with troubled eyes at a lovely wind-tossed sunset.

" Shouldn't have said I'd do it, I suppose," murmured poor Binks. " Only I hate to say no. Georgia would call me a silly! Wish I'd told Georgia all about it. I didn't have any chance to talk to her alone. But I might have made a chance—perhaps. Georgia knows Miss Wales better, and anyway she doesn't mind asking people to do things. Oh—come in!"

The door opened slowly and the poetess, looking tired and out of temper, came in. " I wanted you to go walking," she said reproachfully. "I came at four as usual, and you were out."

"But yesterday I stayed in for you, and you didn't come at all," explained Binks patiently. "And I left a note on the bulletin-board about to-day."

"You know I never look at the bulletin-board," returned the poetess sadly.

"But you ought to," began Binks, and stopped short. "Never mind. Let's not bother over what's past. Do you want to go walking some more, or would you rather just sit here and watch the sunset?"

Miss Ellison stared gloomily out the window. "I'm too tired to walk any more. That divan looks awfully comfortable."

Binks, who was sitting on the divan, stood up politely. "It is. Did you want to write, perhaps? Because if so, I'll go away."

The poetess sank gracefully down among the cushions, pillowing her cheek in one white hand.

"I've put paper out here in plain sight," Binks told her, "and please try not to spill the ink. Good-bye."

"Don't stay too long," commanded the

poetess dreamily. " I shall want to read things to you a little later."

" All right," Binks promised, and hurried off to find Georgia.

" I want to ask you to do something for me," she began abruptly.

Georgia frowned at the stupid mistake she had made about Binks's unworldliness, and shut the door. " Is it about Dramatic Club ? " she asked. " Because you know, Binks,—or rather I suppose you don't know,—that girls are not supposed to ask any member to help them get in. But I don't mind telling you that I'll do my best for you, and I think all the others will."

Binks waited patiently for Georgia to finish. " I understand that, Georgia," she began. " I mean that I know, even though I am rather out of things here, that it's not Harding custom to act as if you wanted to be in anything. You must just pretend you don't care. I try to act that way, but I can't, about things that I really do want."

Georgia looked troubled. " But, Binks, it will queer you hopelessly if you give yourself away about Dramatic Club. Promise me solemnly that you won't ask anybody else to help pull you in."

Binks sighed. "I've got to go back in a minute, and I came about something special. Dramatic Club isn't a thing I really do want, Georgia. Why, I don't know enough about it to think whether I want it or not. But I've discovered something again, and I'm such a 'fraid cat that I thought maybe you'd tell Miss Wales—that is, if you think she ought to know."

Georgia looked hard at her queer little cousin. "Go ahead and tell me," she said, after a long stare of amazed incredulity. "Go ahead and tell me, and I'll tell Betty, if that's what you want. But of all innocent, simple-minded, dense ——" Georgia paused. The degree of Binks's densely innocent simple-mindedness could not be put into words.

"Well," began Binks intently, without noticing Georgia's muttered epithets, "you know the way I always get mixed up with freaks—the way I did last year at the infirmary, with Mariana Ellison, who writes ——"

"I know—the C. P.," interrupted Georgia hastily.

"C. P.?" repeated Binks questioningly. "Oh, yes, the College Poet. That's the one. And Esther Bond was there, and a scientific prod, named Jones."

"I know—the one with the comical squint," put in Georgia, smiling at the recollection.

"Well, she's got a sister," went on Binks quickly, "a freshman. They thought they had enough money for two, with the junior one's scholarship and what she earns tutoring. And then they found they hadn't, and the Student's Aid doesn't generally help freshmen." Binks frowned. "You can't blame the poor things. The junior got Miss Wales to give her a loan, and then she passed it over to her sister. And now after it's gone and she can't pay it back, it has worried her so that she's about sick, and Dr. Carter wants her to give up tutoring and get another loan to carry her through the term.

"And she wouldn't! She came to me and told me and cried, and I said—well, I suppose I promised to fix it up. Wasn't that foolish, when I can't even explain it to you so that it sounds plausible? Why, I've actually left out both her best excuses for doing what looks so dishonest! One is that she could honestly say she needed the loan herself, because she did. She's gone without enough to eat lots of times this year. The other is that the freshman is awfully bright and not very strong, and if her uncle —— Goodness, I forgot to say that an uncle promised to help the freshman, and then, after she'd given up her country school and come to Harding, he backed out. Don't you think there is a good deal of excuse for her, Georgia? Of course the freshman isn't to blame at all, because she didn't, and doesn't know where her sister got the money. There! That's another point I forgot to bring in in its proper place."

"You have got a rather disorderly mind, Binks," admitted Georgia. "You've entirely left out the point that interests me most of all. Why did Miss Jones tell you her story?"

"Oh, I don't know," returned Binks plaintively. "I never know why people tell me queer things. Of course you understand that she had to tell somebody to get it off her mind. And now I've got it off my mind, and I must go right back home. Miss Ellison might be waiting for me."

"Let her wait," advised Georgia coolly. "Did Miss Jones tell you to do as you thought best with her unpleasant little tale?"

Binks nodded.

"Well, are you sure we hadn't better just smother it?"

Binks's small face took on a curiously scornful expression. "Of course we hadn't better smother it. She told me, so that I'd tell the right ones and have it fixed right, so that she can feel honest again. You see,"—she sighed—"those freaks always think that I will know how to fix things—and I never do know. But I can find out," added Binks serenely. "I'm bright enough to do that. Only it is an unpleasant story, and you know Miss Wales, and how to tell it to her right. I think—I'm sure you'd better tell her, Georgia, if you'll be so kind."

"Certainly," said Georgia. "Betty's undoubtedly the one to handle it. I'll see her some time to-morrow."

"Oh, thank you, Georgia." Binks glanced anxiously at her watch and slipped on her ulster. "Perhaps I can do something for you some day. I do wish I could."

"Nonsense," said Georgia bluffly. "I'm not doing anything. Good-bye."

"Good-bye." Binks paused uncertainly on the threshold. "I forgot to say that I don't think the freshman sister should stay on here, even if she had the money. I think she is really ill."

"Dr. Carter thinks so, you mean?" asked Georgia.

"Dr. Carter hasn't seen her. I think so myself. Mother is great on germs, you know, and I've learned to notice when people look ill. The freshman sister is pale and thin, and she coughs just a little, and she works on her nerves—much too hard. She ought to live outdoors for a while and get rested up and fed up. And if she would do that, why perhaps Mother would know of a free sanitorium that takes in—whatever she has. I must go now."

Little Binks hurried eagerly off to conciliate the impatient poetess, leaving Georgia to meditate upon her peculiar cousin and the pathetic story she had told.

"To have people think you're not honest!" reflected Georgia. "I remember something about that from my freshman year. It's pretty bad. But to know yourself that you haven't been honest—that must be just perfectly dreadful. Poor thing! In a way it was all right, too. That makes it even harder. And it's abominably hard not to have any of the things that most girls have here so much too much of. Why, that squint of hers is enough to make her think crooked, and be discontented with life! And if the sister is so done up that she has to leave, then the dishonesty will have been all for nothing. Poor Betty! She won't think I'm much of a rescuer when I dump this bundle of bothers into her nice, comfortable lap."

CHAPTER VIII

JISTS AND SUFFRAGISTS

"You can get a thing off your mind easily enough by telling it to somebody," said little Binks Ames very soberly. "But it isn't so easy to get it off your heart. I don't know how to begin, and I hate to bother you and Miss Wales any more, Georgia, but something has simply got to be done for that poor freshman Jones."

"Didn't your mother know of any free sanitorium?" demanded Georgia.

Binks shook her head. "It costs seven dollars a week at the one she ought to go to, and she'd probably have to stay a year. Seven times two is fourteen and seven times five is —— Oh, dear, I can't do it in my head!"

"Three sixty-four," computed Georgia rapidly. "More than it would probably cost her to stay on here for a year. And that was more than she's got. Can't she get well at home?"

"Maybe," said Binks absently, "but she's a lot surer to at the sanitorium. Georgia, you remember the day you asked me for tea at the Tally-ho? It was full, and everybody seemed to be having a good deal to eat. Your bill for six—I couldn't help seeing it—was two dollars and ten cents."

"It was," said Georgia, "and I had to borrow the ten cents of Fluffy Dutton. Why will you unkindly recall that embarrassing incident, Binks?"

Binks smiled politely at Georgia's little joke. "I was just thinking—if that tea-shop is full every afternoon, and each girl spends thirty or forty cents for tea and cakes, why, in a week they must pay out nearly three hundred dollars."

"Easily," agreed Georgia. "And incidentally they ruin their digestions and their appetites for campus dinners, and we have to eat warmed-up left-overs for next day's lunch. But Betty Wales and her tea-shop flourish, and everybody is happy."

"I was wondering," went on Binks soberly, "if the girls wouldn't be glad to give away more than they do, if they could see that it was really needed. Forty cents for tea doesn't mean anything to most of them. Now wouldn't they give forty cents each to help Miss Jones get well?"

Georgia shook her head slowly. "No, because it's not amusing. Tea and cakes, ordered off stunty menus, served among the extra-special features of the Tally-ho, with your little pals beside you, and a senior you're crazy about at the next table—that's forty cents' worth of fun, or four hundred cents' worth, if you happen to have it. But when you're asked to give away forty cents, it looks as big and as precious as forty dollars. It seems as if it would buy all the things you want, and as if, when it was gone, you'd never see another forty cents as good as that one."

Georgia paused triumphantly, and Binks sighed acquiescence. "All right. You know how things are here, Georgia, and I don't. They won't give the money to Miss Jones, but they'd spend it fast enough at an amusing benefit performance for her. Is that what you mean, Georgia?"

Georgia smiled pleasantly. "No, I didn't

mean that, but it's true, now that you mention it. You're too rapid for me, Binks. I didn't know you were such a rusher. But you go right ahead with your show—that's the Harding term for an amusing benefit performance—and I will stay behind and attend to such practical details as time, place, and the kind permission of the faculty, also the valued approval and assistance of Miss B. Wales. Blood will tell, Binks. You're going into this thing with all Aunt Caroline's fine enthusiasm for good works."

"That freshman Jones is so pathetic," said Binks simply. "If she was my sister I presume I should steal, if necessary, to get her what she needed."

"Gracious, Binks!" protested Georgia. "You sound like a dangerous anarchist."

"Well, fortunately she's not my sister," Binks reassured her cousin, "so I can just help get up a show for her. What kind of a show would it better be, Georgia?"

Georgia laughed. "You speak as if shows grew on bushes, Binks, and we could pick off any kind we liked the looks of. Whereas the sad fact is that we shall have to snatch joyously at any kind we can think of—if we're lucky enough to think of a kind."

"A suffrage bazaar would be rather nice, wouldn't it?" Binks suggested casually. "It would be comical all right, if it was anything like the real ones. Suffragettes are certainly funny, and antis are even funnier."

"Sort of a take-off on the strenuous female, you mean?" inquired Georgia.

Binks nodded. "We could have speeches and a play, if anybody could write one, or maybe a mock trial, and then everybody could vote on the suffrage question. Women's colleges are always voting on suffrage nowadays. They seem to like it."

"That's good, so far," Georgia agreed approvingly. "Why not satirize a few other feminine fads while you're in the business? I can think of a lovely parody on æsthetic dancing. My mother and sisters are going crazy about that."

"We could have a fresh-air children's chorus," Binks added promptly. "I mean children brought up to go barefoot and sleep outdoors in winter and all that sort of foolishness."

"With a special number about women that get up early and walk barefoot in the dewy grass," put in Georgia eagerly.

"And we could have a home-beautiful monologue."

"Never mind going any further, Binks," Georgia told her firmly. "There is evidently no lack of material for an extra-special show entitled Jists and Suffragists."

"Jists?" repeated Binks blankly.

"Jists—jests, jokes. Didn't you ever hear of a merry jist, my peculiar young cousin from Boston?"

"Well, I have now," said Binks imperturbably. "And it will be no merry jist at all if I'm not on hand at four to go walking with the Poetess. So I must rush home. You think the faculty and Miss Wales will be sure to approve, don't you?"

"Oh, yes, I'm sure they will, but you'd better not assign the jist and suffragist parts to your little friends until you hear from me," advised Georgia. "It's considered good form not to be too sure in advance of faculty permits."

When Binks had gone, Georgia lay back on

her broad window-seat and chuckled. "She's all right, is my peculiar cousin," Georgia reflected. "Jists and Suffragists will drag her into Dramatic Club without any help from me. And she doesn't know it. She wouldn't care if she did know it. And I almost let Clio Club get her, just because she was in the family and so I never appreciated her! Well, I appreciate her now. I guess I'll go and find Betty and get her to come with me to see Miss Ferris about the extra-special show."

Never in the whole history of Harding College had there been a more successful affair than Binks's altogether impromptu, go-as-you-please Benefit Performance. Binks's method of arranging the various stunts was quite simple.

"Is your mother a club-woman?" she demanded of each prospective head of a committee. "Well, is she a fresh-air fiend? Or a Suffragette? Or does she go in hard for exercise? She does? Then won't you please be Georgia's right-hand man on her committee? Georgia is getting up some killing kind of a dance, to make fun of the exercise business.

"Now, Susanna, you were brought up on fresh air, and you can write songs. Write one for a chorus of fresh-air-brought-up children, won't you? You can choose your own chorus to sing the song, and consult with them about costumes and all that sort of thing."

It worked like a charm, Binks's method.

"You see," Fluffy explained it, "a clever girl is sure to have a clever mother, and nowadays all clever mothers have fads. Ours has the no-breakfast fad. Straight is trying to write a one-act tragedy entitled, 'Before Breakfast, Never After.' It will be tragic all right if it goes the way I felt the summer that I obligingly tried to join the anti-breakfast crusade." Fluffy, who was engaged at the moment in eating a particularly hearty breakfast at the Tally-ho, returned happily to her second order of waffles.

Of course the B. C. A.'s heard about the extra-special show, and Madeline, who was still in Harding celebrating the acceptance of her novel, could not resist the lure of a project so congenial. She wrote Binks a modest little

note offering to write a one-act farce entitled,
" Waiting Dinner for Mother; or, The Meal-
Hour and the Artistic Temperament."

" It will be founded on my personal observations," Madeline wrote, " and maybe it will
be amusing, because living in Bohemia New
York used to be very amusing indeed, in
spite of too much artistic temperament getting
into the cooking. I think our post-graduate
crowd would act it out for me, and then I
shouldn't be making you any bother."

" Bother!" repeated Binks, reading the
note, which she had just picked off the bulletin-board, aloud to a circle of friends.
" Bother! She's written a play for Agatha
Dwight—a really-truly play that you sit in
two dollar seats to see. And she hopes it
won't be a bother if she writes one for this
show!" Binks, who was not yet a recognized
celebrity, nevertheless leaned against the
sacred note-room table, quite overcome by the
splendor of Madeline's offer.

" Just the same," she told a crowd of committee chairmen later, " we've got to begin refusing things. We've got all we can make
room for now, and every one is just splendid."

"'Ten Numbers. All Top-Liners and One Above the Line. A Play by the Celebrated Miss Ayres. Entertainment Stimulating, Refreshing, Satisfying. Cuisine the Same.' How's that for a scare-head poster?" inquired Susanna Hart blandly.

"Great!" Georgia told her. "But Madeline's play won't be the only real sensation. Wait till you see Eugenia Ford in our Rag Doll Dance. She's a wonder."

"Wait till you see the willowy Mariana Ellison shivering around in the light and airy costume of a Fresh-Air Child."

"Wait till you see Fluffy starring as the Hungriest Daughter in Straight's tragic drama, entitled 'Before Breakfast, Never After.'"

"Wait till you see the whole extra-special show." Thus Binks tactfully suppressed too-ardent rivalries. "Isn't it just too glorious for anything the way everybody takes hold?"

"It would be too glorious for anywhere but Harding College," Georgia told her eager little cousin. "You're getting on to Harding ways pretty fast these days, Binks Ames."

Binks smiled absently. "Am I?" she asked. "I'm having a lovely time, and not studying

any too much, and Miss Ellison thinks I'm
neglecting her and her poems. But I think the
freshman Jones is worth it. It's too bad that
she can't have the fun of the show too; but I
thought it would make her feel queer afterward, when we tell her about the money's
being for her, if she'd taken part in her own
show." Binks smiled again, her sweet, in-
quiring smile. " Another queer thing about
Harding is that nobody thinks what a show is
for."

" If they like it," added Georgia promptly.
" Remember that, Binks, after you're out in
the wide, wide world, and you can be a wonderful help to Aunt Caroline. Aunt Caroline
can supply the Worthy Causes, and you can
match them with Likable Shows."

" Likable " was a mild word for Binks's first
effort, whose " Top-Liner " features filled the
big gym. to overflowing all through the afternoon and evening appointed for it by the
faculty committee. It would easily have filled
the gym. for another afternoon and evening ;
nobody who went had time to see everything
properly, and those who were crowded out of
Madeline's farce or Georgia's Rag Doll and

Ploshkin Dance fairly wept with rage and disappointment. But the faculty set their faces sternly against repetition.

"And I don't wonder," said honest little Binks, "if everybody's work has slumped the way mine has."

But even the faculty enjoyed the show; possibly they enjoyed it a little more than any one else. The Suffrage Bazaar occupied the big stage at the end of the gym. Once in twenty minutes the bazaar "woke up," as the program picturesquely phrased it; and everybody who was not in one of the small side-rooms or curtained alcoves enjoying a side-show, curled up on the floor in a sociable company to see the Suffragettes militantly compel the Antis to buy the useful or beautiful articles they had for sale, such as manacles for tyrannous males, automatic baby-tenders, cookless cookers, and other devices likely to come handy in a home whose head spent her days in Woman's-Club-land. The Suffragettes' persuasive arguments frequently developed into harangues in behalf of the cause. The Antis, who were all timid, pretty creatures, tried to reply, but were speedily heckled down by the pointed questions and comments of their more eloquent opponents. But when a Mere Man appeared, it was the Antis who got possession of him, without any argument at all; and who bore him off to buy violets and chocolate sundaes, pink pin-cushions, purple sofa cushions, and all the other bits of useless frippery that clutter the traditional bazaars gotten up by old-fashioned women. Just before the last Suffragist had lapsed into discouraged silence, a small but determined army of pretty freshmen in Swiss peasant costume swarmed out upon the gym. floor with trays of alluring French cakes and Tally-ho candies, also alluring. And if you stopped to buy those, there was a "House Sold Out" sign in front of Madeline's play; and if you hurried to the play, why, you were likely to go to your grave regretting a certain little cake, with chocolate-covered sides, a pyramid of marshmallow on top spread over with jam, and nobody knew what inside it, that you hadn't stopped to buy.

It sent you into hysterics to see Mariana Ellison, clad in a scant white dress, white stockings, and black ties, throwing cotton snowballs at other tall, scantily attired children, while they all sang a lusty chorus about being cold and well and happy to the tune of "A Hot Time." But if you waited to see them do it again, you missed that mirth-provoking parody on æsthetic dancing, in which twelve Rag Dolls and twelve Ploshkins flopped through a bewitching ballet, the "jist" of which was that the Ploshkins courted the Rag Dolls ardently until the Rag Dolls, remembering that they were new women, turned from pursued to pursuers—and pricked themselves painfully on the Ploshkins' prickly, slippery tails.

"Well," said Binks when it was all over, "I guess they all had a good time."

"Too good for the money," Georgia told her, "but that's a general failing of Harding shows, so don't take it to heart. And as for profits,—I guess the freshman Jones can pass the rest of her life in a sanitorium if she wants to."

"Miss Wales is going to arrange about that," explained Binks. "She went to see her to-night and told her about the plan, and Miss Jones is delighted—of course, because

Miss Wales put it so nicely. Oh, I almost
forgot! Miss Wales brought me a note from
her freshman—Miss O'Toole. I stuck it into
my shirt-waist." Binks felt for the note and
tore it open, whereupon five yellow bills fell
out at her feet.

"A hundred dollars! Whew!"

"Fifteen weeks more paid for at that sanitorium!"

"Hurrah for Montana Marie!"

"Didn't you ask her to take part, Binks?"

"What does she say about the money,
Binks? Hurry up and tell us, can't you?"

"I can if you'll give me a chance," Binks
retorted. "She says that she couldn't be a
Rag Doll as Georgia asked her to, because it
would have taken her mind from her work.
But she came to-night, and had a 'swell'
time; and she sends her contribution to the
expenses, and hopes other girls who were too
busy to help as much as they wanted to will
think to do the same. Isn't she the best
ever?" Binks's brown eyes shone softly.
"Can't we print her letter in the 'Argus'
or stick it up on the bulletin-board or something? Lots of girls in this college have stray

hundred dollars or stray five dollars that they simply don't think to give to Miss Wales. If more people would think, more girls could get loans—even some freshmen—and then these dreadful things ——" Binks paused in consternation at the narrow escape she had had from betraying the confidence of the junior Jones.

"If more people would think straight," Georgia came swiftly to her rescue, "why, fewer people would act crooked. Well, I know at least one matron who will think daggers if Fluffy and Straight and I don't dash for home. So keep the rest of your theories for to-morrow, Binks, and come along."

And they went, singing :

"Here's to Miss Marie, Drink her down!
Here's to Miss Marie, Drink her down!
Here's to Miss Marie, She is fresh from gay Paree,
Drink her down, drink her down, drink her down,
    down, down!"

in a fashion at once mocking and admiring.

CHAPTER IX

THE Tally-ho Tea-Shop was going to open a regular catering department. That was Betty's "lovely new idea," which had been her principal reason for coming back to Harding. Through the desperately busy first days of the term it had slumbered; the single-handed management of Montana Marie O'Toole had kept it in the background; the pathetic episode of the Jones sisters had delayed it still further. But when the B. C. A.'s stepped forward to share in the tutoring of Montana Marie, and when Jim Watson appeared to take Betty off on long, refreshing rides, and to remind her, by many small and tactful attentions, that at least one person in the world was tremendously interested in all her ideas and plans and achievements,—then at last did the lovely new idea for the Tally-ho get its innings. Betty took a day off from her freshman and her secre-

147

taryship, to think the whole thing over. Then she called a business meeting of "resident owners," which was Madeline's high-sounding name for herself and Babbie and Betty. Then she wrote to Mr. Morton, and saw to it that Babbie stopped thinking about Mr. Thayer and " the " wedding long enough to write to Mrs. Hildreth. And the next thing, since everybody heartily agreed about the splendor of the new idea, was to begin.

In this connection Betty enunciated another of her amusing business theories. "It's easy enough to make grand and elegant plans," she declared. " But there's a perfectly awful gap between planning and doing. And in business it's only the doing that counts."

"Yes," agreed Babbie solemnly. " Of course we want to wait until we are perfectly sure what is the very best way of starting in."

Betty sighed despairingly. " Oh, Babbie, that's just what I didn't mean ! I meant that the longer we think and consider and wonder how to begin, the longer,—we don't begin," she ended forlornly.

Madeline patted her shoulder comfortingly.

" I understand, if Babbie, the lady of leisure, doesn't. Of course she doesn't! How can she, when she never has to make an opportunity, and then cram herself down its unwilling throat? Begin any old way, Betty. Only begin. I know the catering department will be a big success."

And so Betty began—with Miss Raymond's dinner. Miss Raymond had moved off the campus, and had a dear little house of her own, away up on the top of Oak Hill. Fräulein Wendt lived there with her, and a fat old French woman kept house for them—exactly as she pleased. And just as Betty was ready to open her catering establishment, a famous author from London came to Harding to deliver a lecture, and also to see Miss Raymond, whom he had met years before in England and wanted to meet again. Miss Raymond was giving a dinner for him. Celine's cooking would do beautifully, she told Betty, coming to her to ask if Nora or Bridget knew of a waitress that she could have in for the great occasion. But Celine's waiting and Celine's table-laying—they would strike terror to his orderly English soul.

"I remember the dinners his sister used to give," she went on. "Such perfect ones, with the loveliest flowers and the daintiest menu cards—you know they use menu cards over there, or they used to, where we should have place-cards—and after dinner just one lovely song or some other fascinating bit of entertainment to start the good talk going. If only I weren't so busy! I simply can't think of anything so frivolous as a dinner. Why couldn't that provoking man have waited till the proofs of my new book were finished?"

Betty murmured polite sympathy, and then, when Miss Raymond had once more remembered her errand and looked suggestively at the door that led to Bridget and Nora, she bravely made the fatal plunge. Miss Raymond was a dreadful person to begin a thing on. She was hard to please. She never made allowances. She never explained what she wanted ; she merely expected you to grasp her ideas with no help at all from her. But, as Madeline would have said, Miss Raymond was Opportunity knocking on the door of the Tally-ho Catering Department. A beginning was a beginning. So Betty plunged.

She explained the idea, and then timidly suggested that the new Catering Company should attempt to supply Celine's deficiencies in the matter of decoration and service. And Miss Raymond, with a gasp of relief and a vague, "You know just the sort of charming thing I want," fled joyously back to her neglected proofs, leaving Betty in a very perturbed, very mixed state of mind. She had got her longed-for chance to begin, but experimenting on Miss Raymond and a great English novelist certainly had its little drawbacks. Even Madeline was somewhat over-awed by the great name of the novelist, and Babbie Hildreth was frankly aghast at Betty's daring.

"Couldn't we have started in with a freshman spread?" she asked. "Then, after a year or so, we could work up to the grandeur of Miss Raymond. Aren't you scared to death, Betty, for fear things will go wrong? Imagine how she'd glare at a waitress who didn't pass things to suit her! The poor creature would probably drop her dishes and flee for her very life."

"Not Nora," said Betty stoutly. "I'm

going to do the table myself, and I shall stay
on in the kitchen during dinner to make sure
that things are sent in looking right. Emily
Davis will attend to that part later, but for this
first time ——"

"You are scared to death," cried Babbie
triumphantly. "But you needn't be. It will
be a howling success, that dinner. I feel it
in my bones. And when Miss Raymond is
pleased, she is very, very pleased. It will be
the making of the Tally-ho Catering Department, Betty Wales, and I shall write Mother
that you are the boldest and most fearless
caterer in the whole country, and that she'd
better engage you for our wedding without
further delay."

Betty laughed. "What you will really do
without delay, Miss Hildreth, is to advise me
about the flowers for the table, and the place-
cards. Of course, for such a terribly intellectual party, our usual Tally-ho ideas are all
out of the way."

Babbie nodded thoughtfully. "Of course.
She wants a perfectly dignified dinner. Key-
note : expensive simplicity. Roses in a tall
glass vase, and place-cards engraved with her

family crest if she has one. Color scheme depending upon her china. Or has Celine smashed so much china that we shall have to use ours? You'll have to conciliate the autocratic Celine, Betty; so you'd better be brushing up your French in your idle moments."

"Don't bother with French, but take me on your preliminary scouting trip," amended Madeline. "I have yet to discover the fat foreign cook that I can't conciliate. I love them so, that I instantly win their foolish hearts."

The scouting trip disclosed the fact that Celine was good-natured, if set in her ways. Also, she had not smashed any of the gold and white Raymond-heirloom china. Instead she kept it under lock and key, and Miss Raymond and Fräulein Wendt were compelled to be satisfied with a plebeian, modern blue and white set purchased by command of the thrifty Celine, who had an obsession to the effect that some day Miss Raymond would marry and have a real home of her own. For this happy consummation Celine insisted upon hoarding the ancestral silver, china, and mahogany, sternly refusing to waste what she shrewdly recognized as real treasures upon this make-believe, makeshift housekeeping, divided between a drab little German lady and a distrait and absent-minded professor in petticoats, whom Celine adored and scolded by turns.

" And for ze grand partie, it is all as you wish," she assured Betty magnificently. " It will do them gut—dis grand partie. I will make food for ze god, mam'selle, chust as you wish. Ze mam'selle, she is busy to-day—no count to disturb. She say do as ze little mam'selle wish, and all goes well. Voila ! "

So Babbie bought long-stemmed yellow roses, and borrowed Mary's tallest and slenderest wedding-present vase to put them in. And when Betty demurred a little at the formidable price of engraved crests, Madeline painted the design in red and gold. Then, to amuse herself, she made another set of Tally-ho-ish cards with clever, flippant pictorial take-offs of the guests as decoration, and below leading questions, "just to start the good talk going," she mimicked Miss Raymond gaily.

" I'd like to plan the great Mr. Joram a

dinner," she declared, " a real live American-college-girl dinner, that would make him sit up and like us all. I say, Betty, wouldn't Miss Raymond stand for a little gleam of original-ity ? "

Betty considered, looking troubled. " Of course those cards are terribly clever, and she might like them, but—if she didn't ——"

" Exactly," Babbie took up the tale. " If she didn't, the Tally-ho Catering Department would be done for. Miss Raymond is a woman of the world, Madeline. She met Mr. Joram in formal London society, and she wants to ——"

" Do a perfectly good return engagement," finished Madeline calmly. " All right, only she's wasting the chance of a lifetime. Tell her so, please, Betty, with my compliments. To pay for a Tally-ho-ish dinner, and then get yel-low roses and crests and regular food—it doesn't strike me as a square deal. But if that's what they want, that's what we furnish. I must de-sign a Tally-ho Catering Department folder, explaining that we are all things to all men, from a dignified dinner without features for Miss Raymond to a Stocking Factory Twelfth

Night Masque, all features, for Mr. Thayer. By
the way, Betty, we ought by rights to have begun on Mr. Thayer."

"He's too busy getting ready to be married,"
laughed Betty. "He isn't interested in factory
parties this year."

"Oh, dear, that's because of me," explained
Babbie sadly. "But even a philanthropist
has to be absorbingly interested in his new
house and his approaching wedding and his
honeymoon. After that,"—Babbie sighed
joyously,—"after that you'll have to help us
and the Stocking Factory to live happy ever
after. And we shall give lots of stunty parties, and we shall need lots of catering, with
features."

"Catering without features charged extra,"
Madeline read from the folder she was busily
composing, "to compensate the company for
the loss of their customary diversions."

"Madeline!" sighed Babbie resignedly.
"What perfect foolishness! You know features are great bothers to think up."

"Also great fun," retorted Madeline. "And
I'll bet you a cookie—a frosted one of Cousin
Kate's—that even the intellectual Miss Ray-

mond would like some features, if she only stopped to consider the matter."

" But we can't be sure that she would," Betty explained again patiently. " And so isn't it safer to act like any other Catering Company and stick to the Dignified Dinner program? "

" Certainly," Madeline agreed promptly. " Keeping my terribly clever place-cards concealed about your person, and my latest Palmist and Crystal gazer stunt on the other end of the Tally-ho's telephone line. But I bet you a dozen Cousin Kate's cookies that if she is given her choice, Miss Raymond will vote for the features."

" I probably shan't see her until after dinner," Betty explained. " So she can't be given her choice. But I'll take the clever place-cards along. And if you can read palms, Madeline Ayres, begin on mine."

" Oh, please do mine first," begged Babbie, " and tell me all about my wedding and after. Why didn't you tell us before that you could read palms? "

" Because I learned only last week," Madeline defended herself coolly, and then proceeded to read all Babbie's future in the lines of her soft little hands in a manner that Babbie and Betty agreed in characterizing as "just perfectly wonderful."

The Dignified Dinner was to be at seven. At six Betty arrived to arrange the yellow roses, dispose the crested place-cards according to Miss Raymond's orders, and make sure that Celine was doing her part and that Nora understood what hers was to be.

"My mam'selle is making ze letter in ze libraire," Celine told her disconsolately. "She belong in ze chambre making ze toilette. Voilà! What is it to be done?"

"The salad—for us," laughed Betty, and Celine joined in good-naturedly, only stopping now and then in the construction of the salad to reconnoiter in her mam'selle's quarters and to lament that "ze toilette" was even yet not begun.

But at quarter to seven Miss Raymond, "ze toilette" completed, though rather sketchily, hurried into the kitchen.

"Oh, Miss Wales," she began, "is everything ready? Did I tell you about the seating? Did I tell you that Professor Francis isn't coming? So now I want Mrs. Merwin opposite Mr. Joram." She swept back to the table. " It's very pretty," she said, gazing absently from the roses to the crests. " These cards are beautifully done. Did I ask you to plan music or something of the sort for later ? But of course that's not catering. I'm as nervous to-night as a freshman before mid-years— and as stupid. I simply haven't had one minute to think since last Sunday. Do I look fit to be seen, Miss Wales? Oh, thank you. Hooking the hostess up isn't catering either, but you do it so well. I'll run up and find a pin to put into that lace in one minute. But first tell me, are any of my guests musical? Have they any parlor tricks? Intellectual dinners are such bores, Miss Wales, unless they're made to be distinctive somehow."

Overwhelmed by the tide of questions, Betty ran over the guest list without finding any one whose " parlor trick " she knew.

" I'm sorry," she faltered. " I didn't know you wanted me to plan any entertainment. I thought ——"

" Oh, never mind," Miss Raymond cut in abruptly. " The table is very nice and Ce-

line's cooking—it's all right, Miss Wales, only
I'd dreamed of something—what is it that
you girls say?—stunty. Something that
would be like your tea-shop, and that would
give Mr. Joram a whiff of the informal, amusing college atmosphere. I ought to have said
so plainly. I never make myself clear." Miss
Raymond sank into the nearest chair with an
air of complete discouragement.

For one little minute Betty hesitated.
Then she flew to the kitchen and returned
with the terribly clever place-cards, which had
been packed in the basket with Mary's vase.

"I'll bring you down a pin," she volun-
teered, "if you'll tell me where to find one.
Meanwhile look these over and see if you
care to use them. Madeline—Miss Ayres—
sent them on the chance. And if you wanted
a splendid palmist and crystal-gazer for after
dinner, you could have her. The costume is
East Indian, with a mystic veil. We would
have asked sooner, only we thought—we were
afraid——" Betty fled, blushing. There was
no use waiting for directions about the pin, because Miss Raymond was bestowing her un-
divided attention upon the new place-cards.

SHE PEEPED CAUTIOUSLY IN AT THE DOOR

When Betty came back five minutes later she peeped cautiously in at the door to discover Miss Raymond happily engaged in rearranging the table, chuckling softly to herself as she moved about. Betty, who had found Fräulein Wendt and a pearl and amethyst pin, came timidly forward. Miss Raymond looked up at her with an expression of girlish gaiety that made you forget that she was ever cold and distant and hard to please.

"My dear child," she said, "you've made my dinner! These cards hit them all off to the life. Nothing else will matter after such a good start, but bring on your crystal-gazing palmist. Put her in the little red sitting-room. Arrange things as you like. And— Mr. Joram will want to meet Miss Ayres. Couldn't you ask her to come up later this evening?"

Betty started to explain that Miss Raymond must choose between Madeline and the crystal-gazing palmist, and then remembered the point Madeline had made of the mystic veil that was to keep her interestingly anonymous.

So, " I'm afraid she can't come to-night,

Miss Raymond," Betty explained demurely. "That is, not until very late. I—I think she's engaged for to-night."

" Then I want to engage your catering company for another dinner next week, when Mr. Joram comes back. I'll let you know the night, and Miss Ayres must come then for dinner."

Three hours later Betty, tired but triumphant, was assisting the crystal-gazing palmist to extract the pins from the entangling meshes of her mystic veil. The crystal-gazing palmist was also triumphant. Nobody had pierced the disguise of the mystic veil. Miss Raymond had told Mr. Joram all about that queer amusing Miss Ayres, who stopped writing plays for Agatha Dwight to design candle shades for the Tally-ho Tea-Shop. Mr. Joram had inquired sotto voce of the palmist if faculty dinners at Harding were always like this one. Miss Ferris had blushed ignominiously when the palmist found a wedding within a year in her hand. Best of all, George Garrison Hinsdale—Mary fortunately was spending the week with Babe—had assured the palmist solemnly that her character readings were " simply stunning. "

"It wasn't a very dignified dinner," said Betty, pulling out the last pin, just as a fresh burst of laughter floated out from the rooms in front.

Madeline smiled. "Rather not—nor intellectual. But they've had a good time. By the way, may I collect my cookies as I go home? I've decided to sit up and write for a while, and I shall need midnight refreshments."

"Of course you can have them or anything else we've got," Betty promised gratefully. "Oh, Madeline, you are a jewel! Just suppose we hadn't had any substitutes for crests and— and—dignity."

Madeline yawned. "Before I write the play that I'm going to do to-night," she announced casually, "I'll amend our advertising circular. I'm going to cross out 'Catering without Features charged extra,' and say 'Catering without Features may be had elsewhere.'"

"But that will sound fearfully unbusinesslike," Betty protested.

"Business," began Madeline dogmatically, "is the art of putting your best foot forward. Our best foot is features. Business is giving the people what they want. They all want features, even the touch-me-not Raymonds and the high and mighty Jorams. Ergo —— " she waved her mystic veil convincingly. " You began with features, Betty. You're therefore committed to features. And I, crystal-gazing palmist and seeress of renown, prophesy that the Tally-ho Catering Department will succeed beyond our wildest dreams, with features. Now come and help me find those cookies."

CHAPTER X

PRE-CHRISTMAS excitements and Christmas gaieties were alike things of the past. Harding was bleak and snow-bound in the clutches of a real old-fashioned New England January. And the college cynics declared gloomily that the cold and forbidding weather was a symbol of cold and unforgiving faculty hearts.

" There are too many of us," sighed Straight, who was more worried than she cared to admit over her record in junior argument. " Prexy thinks this college is getting too big. Maybe it is, but can't they wait till next year to have it get smaller? It's rather hard on us, I think, to try to crowd us out, just because they calmly let in such a huge mob of freshmen."

" Well, the whole huge mob wanted to come and passed its exams all right," argued Fluffy. " So how could it be lawfully kept out? But imagine the freshmen's states of mind about

165

now, poor things, with all these horrid rumors flying around. Why, if I were a this year's freshman I believe I should give up the game and end my days in a boarding-school."

"You would!" sniffed Straight. "You're a nice one to sympathize with frightened freshies. You never got warned in your life!"

"Well, just the same I've been scared times enough," demurred Fluffy. "Being scared hasn't anything to do with a good reason for being scared, specially not for freshmen."

"Maybe you're right," said Straight reflectively. "I've seen several prods act speechless with fright, but I always thought it indicated that they weren't genuine prods at all,—only clever bluffers."

"You mean me for one, I suppose," said Fluffy cheerfully. "Now just to show you that I'm a really-truly prod and no bluffer, I'll take you home and tell you about a priori argument. And then maybe you'll have a little more respect for the high quality of my brains."

Montana Marie O'Toole shared keenly in the prevalent mood of depression. Her radiant smile was dimmed.; her cheerful interest in each and every aspect of college life waned. She concentrated her mind on her work so violently that she grew pale and thin under the strain. Betty and the Concentrating Influence united in protests against the wanton sacrifice of so much youth and beauty; but Montana Marie stood firm.

"It's now or never for little me. I'm bright enough to see that far in front of me," she told them with forced gaiety. " I guess I can better afford to lose a little sleep and exercise than I can to risk failing in these awful mid-years."

A little tremor of fright and nervous dread shook Miss O'Toole's fine shoulders, and Betty, feeling that she had been pushing her protégée much too hard, took her out for a walk and a merry dinner at the Tally-ho, at which kind-hearted Fluffy poohed at mid-year terrors, Madeline Ayres led Marie on to reminisce of dear old Paree, Babbie Hildreth won her heart by asking advice about bridesmaids' dresses, and the mirth of the company in general left her utterly forgetful of math., Latin prose, and English One, of concentration, mid-years, and the strenuous life of a conditioned freshman.

" I've had a perfectly grand time," she told Betty, as they parted in the corridor at Morton Hall. " Gracious, but I do love a good time. I'd like to do nothing but enjoy myself for one solid week. I shan't work so hard after mid-years are over—if I'm not over then too." Marie's laugh at her own joke was rather spiritless, and her expression grew suddenly serious. For mid-years would not be over for another two weeks, and Mrs. Hinsdale's long round of visits had resulted disastrously to progress in Latin prose. Connie could not help with that, but she was splendid about the originals in solid geometry.

" If I owned a school," Marie told her gratefully, " I'd hire you and Mrs. Hinsdale and Miss Mason, and I guess Miss Adams, to teach there. Only of course Miss Adams wouldn't leave Harding, and Mrs. Hinsdale couldn't leave her husband, and Miss Mason is going to Germany next year to study. But you'd come, wouldn't you? Only of course I don't own a school, and I don't suppose I ever shall."

"I'm just as much obliged for your offer," Connie told her brightly. "Now you'd better go right to bed and get well rested. It's less than a week before you'll have to begin to cram."

"What in the world do you mean by cram?" inquired Marie blankly.

Connie explained, and Marie gave a despairing sigh. "Blanket your windows, or get a special permit from the matron, drink coffee, tie a wet towel around your head, and study till three A. M.," she repeated aghast. "Well, I guess I will go right to bed. Just the thought of this cramming prospect makes me tired. Is it compulsory?"

Connie explained the official disapproval of cramming, and then quoted the famous rhyme about the luckless wight who

"did not hurry
Nor sit up late to cram.
She did not even worry
But—she failed in her exam."

"I see," said Montana Marie briefly. The next morning she went down-town and bought a copper coffee-maker. It matched her chafing-dish, added greatly to the elegance of her tea-table, and was the envy of every Morton Hallite. Montana Marie listened politely to the popular chorus of admiration, and said nothing about the real reasons which had actuated her extravagant purchase.

Betty Wales knew nothing about the coffee-maker, or Connie's ideas on cramming; but she was quite as worried about her protégée's prospects as Montana Marie could possibly be herself.

"The poor thing is perfectly sure she's going to flunk," she told the B. C. A.'s at a special tea-drinking called by Mary to discuss the impending crisis.

"Oh, well, so is every freshman sure she'll flunk," condoled Babbie Hildreth easily, "and most sophomores."

Betty nodded. "Of course. The difference is that the rest won't flunk, except a few who aren't expecting to, and Marie will, I guess, from all that I hear."

The acting tutors exchanged surreptitious glances, and reluctantly agreed that Betty was right.

"Has she really lost her nerve—given up the ship?" asked Madeline thoughtfully.

"Oh, no," Betty told her, "she's trying harder than ever. She's determined to pass."

"She's working too hard, probably," said Mary thoughtfully. "She really knows a good average amount about Latin prose."

"Her themes are fair now," put in Madeline.

"She knows heaps more about freshman lit. than I ever did," acknowledged Helen Adams.

"When she isn't nervous about it she can reason out her geometry pretty well," Christy testified. "She's naturally quite logical."

"Then," said Babbie Hildreth, looking sternly at the official tutors, "if you've done your duty, as you imply that you have, and she's fairly well up in everything, why in the world are you so pessimistic about her exams?"

Mary answered for them all. "She is all right enough when she's only reciting to us, or even in regular class work. But she realizes that the faculty are going to be extrafussy with her, because of her conditions and the general situation. She never passed a formal exam in her life till she came here last year ——"

"And then she flunked more than she passed," put in Madeline flippantly.

"She thinks, like all little freshmen, that everything depends on mid-years, and she'll get nervous and excited, and write utter nonsense," ended Mary, disregarding the interruption.

"Give her soothing syrup," suggested Madeline, who refused to take Montana Marie's troubles seriously. Babbie frowned at her, and then, leaning forward on one elbow, she frowned at space, thinking very hard indeed about the far-away days when she was the prettiest, the idlest, the most reckless, and the cleverest of the famous "B" trio, and had mid-years of her own and Bob's and Babe's to worry about, and plan to scrape through somehow, for the honor of the B's and the "finest class" of 19—. Everybody else was thinking, too, but Babbie was the first to have an articulate idea.

"Why, Babe used to be just that way," she said in a surprised tone. "If she crammed a lot and got to thinking how terrible mid-years are, why, she couldn't do anything. And Bob was just the opposite—never paid attention in class, just dawdled along, and then sat up all night with the text-book for the course and some prod's note-book that she'd borrowed, and next day she could answer anything. After mid-years the faculty always thought they'd misjudged Bob." Babbie giggled cheerfully. " Babe really knew heaps more. We used to have such times persuading her to frivol all mid-year week."

" How'd you do it?" asked Madeline idly.

" Pretended to frivol ourselves. Did frivol some to get her started. Got up anti-cram movements. Insinuated that we weren't going to sit up a single night that year. Oh, it was an awful bother getting Bob a chance to grind and keeping Babe from grinding and tending up to things a little myself," ended Babbie with a reminiscent sigh.

" Well, it's lucky you had such a lot of practice," Mary Brooks Hinsdale told her sweetly, " and that you came back here this week to see about the big fireplace for the Robert Thayers' library. Because you are qualified to act, and are hereby elected to act, as chairman of the committee on the mid-year madness of Montana Marie O'Toole. Betty, the assistant tutors, and everybody else who is needed to divert her mind, are hereby elected to the committee. We'll get that child through yet, Betty Wales ; so please don't look so discouraged."

Betty laughed. " I was only thinking what a stupid I am, not to have planned all this long ago myself. Of course you'll get her through ! Why, I believe you could get a broomstick doll through mid-years."

" We are a clever lot," agreed Madeline complacently. " Well, I must go. Plan the campaign, Babbie, assign parts, and we'll come in strong at the finish. And the finish shall not involve the finish of Montana Marie. Nay, it must not," she went on in melodramatic tones. " Montana Marie is a treasure. To bury her in her native state or to return her to dear distant Paree would be to deprive the Harding firmament of its brightest star— and me of my most treasured understudy for a heroine."

" There she goes again on her Literary Career," cut in Mary scornfully. " Come home with me for dinner, Babbie, and make plans for the great campaign. I almost promised George to go and call on his new assistant this evening, but I, for one, am capable of unselfish renunciation. And the moral of that,"—Mary fastened her furs and linked arms with the submissive Babbie,— " is : when the new assistant is a frump, George really shouldn't ask me to call on her. Good-bye, Betty. If you think best, you might relieve Prexy's mind about his over-conditioned freshman. Not knowing us as well as you do, he may be getting quite desperate."

The thought of mid-year week had been a nightmare to Montana Marie. Studying every minute, sitting up half the night, worrying, hurrying, spending your time on the questions you weren't asked and forgetting the answers to the ones you were—that, in brief, had been her notion of the fatal occasion. But a few days before the ordeal she began to get some new ideas. Betty called her into her cozy room at the Morton to say encouraging things about the effort she was making and to advise her not to overwork. Pretty Babbie Hildreth came to call, said more flattering things about Marie's valuable opinions of bridesmaids' dresses, and hoped, very casually, that she wasn't planning to cram ; it was just a silly freshman trick, and always did more harm than good. Madeline Ayres dragged Marie off to a matinée at the Junction. Helen Adams took her for a walk at the hour appointed for an English lesson.

" And we talked all the way about men," Marie told Connie afterward. " Imagine Miss Adams getting on to that subject ! She knows quite a lot about it, too. I suppose she takes her ideas out of Shakespeare and Thackeray and Scott and the rest of the classics. I've found some of them right here in ' Much Ado about Nothing.' I never thought of finding useful ideas in Shakespeare on a real practical subject like men."

When mid-year week was actually upon her, Montana Marie had no time to grow nervous, or frightened or discouraged, or to overwork. The B. C. A.'s left her mornings and early afternoons undisturbed, save for friendly offers of help from the tutors. But about four there was always some fun afoot. A walk, a skating or snow-shoeing party, a sleigh-ride in Mary's trim cutter,—then a merry dinner at the Tally-ho or the Belden, and after that you were much too sleepy to sit up and study. So Connie and the new coffee-maker retired behind a screen, and Montana Marie slept the dreamless sleep of those who have had their fill of fresh air.

The first examination she pronounced "pretty fierce." The next "wasn't bad." English, she declared, she really enjoyed.

"And what do you think," she told Connie in great excitement, "I got in Shakespeare's ideas about men. I chose it for my theme subject. I may not know much about Shakespeare, but I know a lot about men. I shouldn't be surprised if that theme made a hit."

It did. The freshman English teacher showed it to Miss Raymond, and Miss Raymond read it to a senior theme-class as an example of the value of having something to say before you tried to say it.

And so Montana Marie O'Toole passed through the ordeal of mid-years unscathed save for a low-grade or two.

"And what is a low-grade or two?" inquired Babbie scornfully. "Even prods get those."

" I've learned a lot this last week," Montana Marie informed Betty gratefully. " I've learned to do an outer edge on the ice, and to skee—if it isn't too much of a hill. And I've learned what it means to really concentrate your mind. I thought before that it meant to work all the time, just as hard as you can. But it doesn't. It means to work like anything till you're tired, and then play like anything till you're rested. Now that's my style. Me for concentration. Concentration for mine," ended Montana Marie, whose smile had recently got back all its former brilliant radiance.

CHAPTER XI

With mid-years safely behind her, Montana Marie fairly radiated happiness.

"I'm anchored here till June all right, I guess," she giggled joyously. "If I don't do something extra-specially silly, I guess I can certainly stay till June. And now that I've caught on to the rights of this concentration business, why, I can enjoy myself a little. No, I'm not worrying about next near. I never worry about things so far off as next year. Besides, maybe by next year —— " Montana Marie shrugged her shoulders with truly Parisian éclat, and blithely refused to finish her sentence.

Montana Marie's idea of a good time seemed to center around things to eat. She became a Perfect Patron of the Tally-ho, and almost every evening she gave a chafing-dish party in her room. Connie could not afford to waste her evenings over chafing-dish parties, but she was too obliging to complain. So she merely disappeared, just before the parties were due to arrive, spent her evenings studying with the Thorn or reading in the college library, and was unaffectedly delighted when, just as the fudge was cool enough to eat, or the rarebit done to a turn, Montana Marie left her guests to search Morton Hall from top to bottom for her missing roommate.

"The eats are served," she would announce with a giggle, when she had discovered Connie's whereabouts. " We're only waiting for you, so hurry along, and bring all your friends."

Montana Marie could never learn the names of the Morton Hall girls. "They all look alike to me," she declared, and hospitably invited any and all that she met in the corridors to come and have " eats," and meet the Duttons and Georgia and Susanna Hart and Timmy Wentworth. Marie was past-mistress of the difficult art of "mixing crowds." After her advent Morton Hall suddenly took its place as a social center among the other campus houses. The Belden invited the Morton to be its partner in getting up a house play. It was discovered that two of the sophomore basket-ball team lived in the Morton, and one "Argus" editor. The monthly house spreads, which Betty had started in the interests of general sociability, suddenly blossomed out into popular campus functions. The Morton Hallites were learning to play as well as they worked, and it was Montana Marie O'Toole who had taught them. Betty Wales smiled as she remembered how hard she had tried to keep Marie out of the house.

"I guess it's generally the best plan to let things sort of decide themselves," she reflected. "Then if they go wrong, you can blame it on the things, and with me, anyway, they usually go right—only there are some things that just won't decide themselves." Betty Wales was not thinking of the Tally-ho Catering Department (which was deciding to be the howling success that Babbie had predicted), nor of the Student's Aid Secretaryship, nor of Montana Marie O'Toole, among whose faults was certainly not to be ranked a lack of decision.

"Oh, goodness me!" said Betty Wales at last to the open fire in her cheerful sitting-room at Morton Hall. "A girl ought to know her own mind. I'm old enough to know what I want. I'm grown up. But I don't feel a bit grown up. I just hate flirts. It's perfectly dreadful to keep a nice man on the string. But he won't let me say no—and I'm not ready to say yes—not to anybody —yet."

The little Student's Aid Secretary put on an old skirt, a white sweater, and a fuzzy white cap, and went off for a solitary tramp in the snow.

"Anyhow it's better to wait till you're quite sure what you want than to decide wrong and be very unhappy about it afterward," she thought, as, looking very young and irresponsible and contented once more, she shook the snow out of her hair and hurried in to her place at the head of a Morton Hall dinner table.

Montana Marie O'Toole was not at dinner that evening. After having been for two days without ready money she had received a check in the afternoon mail and had promptly sallied forth to find friends who would help her spend it. But for some unknown reason

the afternoon seemed to be a busy one for
all the college but Montana Marie. Fluffy
was writing a long over-due lit. paper;
Straight was coaching the sophomore basket-
ball team; Georgia had disappeared directly
after lunch, nobody knew where; Eugenia
Ford was just starting for chemistry lab.;
Timmy Wentworth had promised to go skating. Finally Montana Marie gave up in
despair and wended her solitary way toward
her bank. She would get the check cashed,
anyway, if she couldn't find anybody to come
and play with her. She would send a lot of
flowers and candy to all her tutors, and buy a
lovely present for Miss Wales. She hadn't
half thanked them all for getting her through
mid-years. She had been too busy tearing
around having a good time. It was lucky
that she had happened to walk down-town
alone, because it gave her a chance to think,
and to remember about all the people she
ought to be grateful to. Montana Marie
arrived at the shopping district of Harding in
a fine glow of remorse and appreciation. She
was just turning the corner to the bank when
she met Dorothy Wales, walking sedately

along in company with another little girl—a fat little girl with twinkling blue eyes and the general flyaway air of having dressed in a hurry.

Dorothy greeted Miss O'Toole with shy politeness, and Montana Marie smiled her most expansive smile in return.

"Come in with me while I get some money," she urged hospitably, "and then we can go down street together."

"I'm afraid we can't," began Dorothy, but the fat little girl overruled her.

"Oh, come on," she urged. "We can run all the way home up that back street."

In the bank, while she waited her turn at the cashier's window, Montana Marie had a thought. "What do you kids want most in the world?" she demanded genially, as they went out.

The fat child had her heart's desire on her tongue's end. "Cream puffs—all I can eat."

Dorothy laughed up into Montana Marie's lovely, smiling face. "How silly, Janet Peyton, to want cream puffs the most of anything," she said reproachfully.

"Well, what do you want most of anything,

dearie?" insisted Marie. Her great thought had been to the effect that the nicest thing she could do for Miss Wales was to make the Smallest Sister blissfully happy. Incidentally it would be fun to fill up fat little Janet Peyton with cream puffs.

Dorothy considered carefully, bound not to rush into silliness.

"If you'd asked me yesterday," she explained at last, "I'd have said a turquoise ring right away, 'cause turquoises are my birth-stone, and all my roommates have got rings with their birth-stones in. But to-day I think I'd rather have a pink sash and pink hair-bows, to freshen up my old white dress for the school party that we're going to have this week. Betty says I don't need a new dress, so I s'pose I don't. But whatever she says, my sash is awfully mussy."

Montana Marie steered her charges into the nearest jewelry store and demanded turquoise rings. Fat little Janet opened her blue eyes in astonishment, and Dorothy blushed very red and picked at Marie's sleeve.

"I can't have one," she explained in an agitated whisper. "I only said I wanted one.

Oh, no, you mustn't get it for me. Betty wouldn't like me to take such a elegant present from you."

Montana Marie patted her shoulder soothingly. "Yes, she would—just a little ring—from me. Your sister is so lovely to me, and there's so little I can do in return. We'll take the littlest ring if you like—there's nothing very elegant about that. Now come along and find the pink ribbons and the cream puffs."

At the big dry-goods store Dorothy again timidly explained that Betty wouldn't want her to take such big presents from any one, and Montana Marie kissed her troubled little face, bought the widest, softest pink sash in the shop, with extra-long hair ribbons to match, pressed the tempting parcel into her hands, and tucked the tiny ring box deep down in her coat pocket.

"Now for cream puffs," she said, smiling at fat little Janet.

"We're awfully late already, Janet," began Dorothy. "Do you think ——"

"Come, don't be selfish," Marie broke in gaily. "You've had your presents, and now it's Janet's turn. You can run home up that back way, you know."

Cuyler's was nearer than the Tally-ho, so they went there. Marie ordered hot chocolate to go with the cream puffs, and ices to cool off on, because they had hurried so, and a German pancake because she had never tried one and wanted to see what it was like. And whenever fat little Janet finished an order of cream puffs, Marie instructed the waitress to bring more. She made the eating of all the cream puffs you wanted seem the most delightful and reasonable thing in the world. Finally fat little Janet smacked her lips over a luscious crusty mouthful, pushed back her plate with a sigh, and said she was through.

"How I'm ever going to run up that hill!" she ruminated sadly. "I've eaten too much, I guess."

"You've just got to run," Dorothy told her firmly, and then she give a little squeal of dismay. "We've forgotten Miss Dick's errand that we came down-town for. We've got to go back by Main Street after all."

"That's good," Montana Marie consoled them, "because now we can go together. I'd take you all the way back to Miss Dick's and explain about my having made you late, only I've just remembered that I have to be tutored in English at half-past four, and it's nearly that now. But you just tell her, Dorothy, that I made you come along with me, and that I'm a friend of your sister's, and she won't scold."

Miss Dick's errand was at a drug store; one of the girls had a bad cold and the school doctor had prescribed for it.

"Want a soda while we wait?" Marie asked Janet.

Janet shook her blond head hard. "No, thank you. It might make us later," she said very solemnly.

"How do you two happen to be down-town without a teacher?" asked Marie curiously. " In the boarding-schools I went to we always walked two and two, with a teacher policing the end of the line."

" Well, you see Harding is such a safe little place," explained Dorothy, " and Miss Dick believes in trusting us a good deal, and——"

" We're both honor girls," cut in Janet placidly.

Montana Marie could not repress a wild peal of laughter.

"You won't bo any longer, I guess," she told them gaily, "but never you mind that. You've had what you wanted most in this world, and that ought to count for something."

Pursuing her policy of showing proper gratitude to those who had helped her to stay in Harding, Marie asked Helen Adams to have dinner with her at the Tally-ho.

Over the desert she told the story of her afternoon adventure. "I wish I knew whether the fat little one is sick from overeating," she said, "and whether Dorothy minded the scolding she probably got. I ought to have thought about the consequences, but I never do for myself, and so I didn't for them. Getting in and out of scrapes is the whole fun of boarding-school, as far as I can see, but those infants said they were honor girls, so I guess they haven't had as much experience with scrapes as I have. Will Miss Wales be awfully cross at me, do you think, for getting her little sister into a mess?"

Uncertainty on this point kept Marie from

asking questions for two days. Then she confided her anxieties to Betty, and persuaded her to go and help find out what had happened when the "honor girls" came home from their belated expedition after medicine.

Dorothy came dancing down-stairs to receive them, flying into Betty's arms, and wiggling hastily out to offer a polite handshake to Marie, who grinned sheepishly, and inquired for Janet.

"She's all right now," Dorothy told her, "but she felt pretty sick that night, and she says she doesn't want any more cream puffs at present and maybe not ever."

"And did you get scolded for being late?" asked Marie hastily.

"Well, yes, we did," explained Dorothy. "But it wasn't your fault a bit, Miss O'Toole. We ought to have said no and stuck to it. Miss Dick said we ought."

"And did she take you off the honor list?" demanded Marie.

"Well, yes, she did," admitted the Smallest Sister reluctantly. "For the present she did. She said she felt that she must, as an example, but that she really thought we could

be trusted pretty soon again. You see," the
Smallest Sister's face was very earnest, "you
don't very often meet somebody who will give
you the things you want the most of all in the
world. We explained all that to Miss Dick,
and she said it was an unusual 'sperience to
have happen. And Betty dear, ought I to keep
the sash and the ribbons and the ring? Miss
Dick said I was to ask you about that. Only
I—I didn't tell her about the ring because—
because I couldn't stand it to have her say I
mightn't keep it," sighed the Smallest Sister
despairingly. "And it's been just awful
waiting for you to come, because Miss Dick
said it would be best for me to wait till you
came, and not on any account to send for
you."

"But wasn't the school party last night?"
asked Marie.

The Smallest Sister nodded. "I wore my
mussy old sash to that."

"So you didn't get quite what you wanted
after all," said Marie when Betty had decided
that Dorothy might keep Marie's presents,
only Marie mustn't do so any more. "You
wanted a sash to wear to the party, and you

only got one you couldn't wear, and I'm awfully sorry about getting you into a scrape with Miss Dick. I was so busy feeling grateful that day that I never thought about anything else."

The Smallest Sister sighed. " It's very hard to think of everything at once, isn't it?" she said quaintly. " Yourself and the person that's with you and the person that's waiting. 'Specially the person that's waiting."

" Very 'specially the person that's waiting," repeated Montana Marie O'Toole, with a burst of merriment quite unwarranted by the Smallest Sister's argument.

Betty Wales blushed a vivid scarlet and looked suspiciously at the mirthful Marie. But Marie was quite unconscious of Betty's indignant scrutiny. Marie was looking blissfully at nothing in particular, and the Smallest Sister was looking in amazement at Marie. Betty Wales's blush had therefore been quite unnecessary, and as soon as she was assured of that it faded as swiftly as it had come.

CHAPTER XII

THE POPPING MASCOTS

LIKE every well-conducted freshman Montana Marie O'Toole took a vast interest in the basket-ball championship. Having been effectually barred from the team by her numerous entrance conditions and her even more numerous fall-term warnings, she was not disappointed, like some of her friends, when the team was chosen. Being an insuperable optimist, she cared not that the sophomore players were known as the Invincibles because they had never lost an interclass match.

When a practical-minded freshman player remarked, " Of course we can't win, but we can play ball," Montana Marie smiled her dazzling smile and retorted, " Don't you give up yet. You can play ball and the rest of us can shriek—yelling is forbidden, they say, in this polite institution. And maybe—well, truth is stranger than fiction," Montana Marie concluded with a cheerful giggle.

From this and many similar speeches the team gradually got the impression that Miss O'Toole had learned some wonderful trick-play in dear old Paree, which she was saving, to make sure that the sophomores didn't get hold of it, until the very last days of team-practice. There was still another rumor to the effect that Montana Marie was as wonderful at basket-ball as at horseback riding, and that the faculty, out of deference to her peculiar position in college, had consented to her joining the team just before the great game, provided that her work until then was kept strictly up to the mark. But when the Invincibles lost two of their starriest stars, all because of mere low-grades in some obscure subject like elocution, the rumor that the scholarship rule was to be stretched for Marie's benefit lost credence. But that she was to be depended upon to do something, certainly interesting and probably effective, nobody seemed to doubt. As Fluffy Dutton remarked, "She's an awful bluffer, but somehow she always comes out on top."

"Yes, she does," agreed Straight, who, as head coach of the sophomore Invincibles, was

peculiarly interested in Montana Marie's proceedings, " and the reason is that nobody can
get a word out of her edgewise. Maybe she
has thought up a grand plan, and maybe she
hasn't an idea in her pretty head. But which-
ever way it is, she just smiles the same old
smile. She's a regular wizard at keeping
secrets, that girl is."

" Then maybe the freshman coaches are
just as near crazy as you are," Fluffy threw
out gaily.

" I'll bet they are," Straight took up her
twin soberly. " I'll bet she has even the
freshman captain guessing. I'll bet the freshman high moguls would go for her good and
hard, if they dared,—for raising false hopes
and getting the team overexcited, and all that
sort of thing. But they don't dare, because
they can't make her out. And there's one
chance in a hundred that she's thought up
the grand plan that will save them."

Straight was a clever forecaster; the situation in the freshman class was exactly as she
had analyzed it. The team lost its temper
and wasted its practice hours discussing the
truth about Montana Marie. The ruling

spirits of the freshman class, who saw the fine esprit de corps of the Invincibles falling in ruins, raged in executive sessions and singly and in groups interrogated the sphinx-like Miss O'Toole. She received their inquiries with smiles, giggles, and blank, non-committal impenetrability.

"I should say we ought to win! Well, rather! Can I do anything to help? Why, really I can't tell you offhand like this. I'll think hard, and maybe I'll have a thought— isn't that what that killing Fluffy Dutton is forever saying? And when I have a thought, I'll let you know."

Thus did Montana Marie O'Toole meet the pointed inquiries of the leading freshmen, and bring their plans for sounding her to naught. Montana Marie O'Toole had entered Harding against all rules and precedents. She had stayed despite the gloomiest prophecies to the contrary. With all her peculiarities she was close friends with the most prominent upper-class girls. She always got what she wanted. She wanted the freshman team to win. "Ergo ——" Timmy Wentworth completed the syllogism with a wave of her good right arm. Timmy, who was coaching the freshmen, was unable to decide whether or not the vague confidence they felt in Marie offset the damaging effect of their constant quarrels about her. But being a lover of the picturesque and the bizarre, Timmy was personally amused by the episode. Also logic is logic.

The winter term wore on its long and tedious course. The weather continued unreasonably cold; so did the hearts of the faculty. The Invincibles lost a third member, their prize home, and the freshmen their best center. However, a sub who had been taken on at the last minute turned out to be quite a wonder at jumping, and on the whole the freshman chances were looking up a little. Finally it was only two weeks to the great game, then ten days, a week, and less than a week. Timmy Wentworth, being consulted by the leading freshmen, advised them to go to Marie once more.

" And this time don't you be so afraid of her," she urged. " Call her bluff. Make her show her hand. If she gets mad about it, never you mind. Trick-plays that she keeps to herself won't help us any. Now is the time for her to come out with her great thought. If she won't—or can't—why, we shall just have to scrape along without it."

So a solemn deputation of six, headed by the class president, waited upon Marie that same afternoon. Marie listened to them with her habitual contemplative smile.

"It is getting pretty near the time, if we're going to spring something good," she agreed vaguely at last. "But say, what makes you all so sure that I can think of the right thing?"

The freshman president referred briefly to the rumors. "Reports like that usually have some truth in them. Besides, you've sort of hinted at something when we've asked you before."

"I have? I've hinted? Well, that's news to me," declared Marie jovially. "I just said that I'd try to think, didn't I, or some pretty speech like that? Well, I—I've been fearfully busy. But of course, if you're depending on me ——" Marie paused to giggle riotously. "I never saw a basket-ball game, you know,—a big one, that is, with lots of people watching and all that. Couldn't we—couldn't we—rattle the other side?"

"How?" demanded the freshman president inexorably.

Marie indulged in her very Frenchiest shrug. "Why, the regular ways, I suppose, only more so."

"That's easy to say," the freshman president objected sternly. "But the Invincibles won't rattle in any regular way. They're too sure of themselves."

"Well, then," said Montana Marie calmly, "it's certainly up to us to think of some unusual ways." She settled herself more comfortably in Connie's easy chair, and passed the inexorable freshman president a box of very expensive chocolates. "Now you folks go ahead and tell me about what happens at a big game. Go into all the details. Then maybe I shall have a thought on the subject of rattling those Invincibles. Fire away now. And keep the chocolates moving."

The president began, rather scornfully. Never having seen a big game herself, she soon found herself somewhat hazy about details. So were the rest of the deputation.

In the end Marie hunted up Connie, who had retired to a quieter spot for the purposes of study; and Connie, who, from much experience, believed in all Montana Marie's strange methods, took up the tale. The team-mascots interested Marie extremely.

" Have we got one fixed up yet? " she demanded.

The deputation explained that they had. It was to be Professor Hart's youngest son, arrayed in " invincible " armor.

Marie nodded approvingly. " What's theirs? "

" We think they've got black Mandy's little Mandy to be it," explained the freshman president. " We don't know how she's going to be dressed."

Marie ruminated. " Does a team ever have more than one mascot? " she demanded at last.

Connie said no. " It would be like carrying a purse full of lucky pennies," she explained primly. " One mascot is enough."

Marie considered. " If there's no rule against more than one," she announced at last, " I think a whole row stuck up in the freshman gallery—popping out one at a time, you know, when things were going against us —would be sort of rattling—if you ask me."

" Where'd you keep them till they popped?" inquired a practical freshman.

Marie shrugged. " Ask Connie."

"In the boxes that the back row of girls stand on, couldn't you?" suggested Connie promptly.

" Of course," agreed the freshman president.

" Well, what could we have for the extra ones?" pursued the practical freshman.

" Class animal," suggested somebody.

" Black Mandy's Jimmie," suggested somebody else. " Little Mandy will curl up and cry when she sees all the people staring at her, but Jimmie would be game for anything."

" It isn't against any rules, is it, for mascots to keep popping out?" asked a cautious girl —she had made herself a leading spirit by saving her class from many of the indiscretions common to impulsive freshman bodies.

Connie, upon being appealed to, could not think of any rule covering the popping out of extra mascots after the great game had begun. " Of course," she said, " Miss Andrews always asks the galleries to sit still and not scream; and near the baskets you can't have your feet over the edge. Those are the only rules I ever heard of."

"Well, we can get around those all right," the freshman president declared easily. "The mascots can pop as silently as ghosts. But if the sophs don't giggle or shriek or make some silly disturbance just as the Invincible home is trying to make a basket, or the center is diving after a new ball—why, then we shan't have the bother of carrying you around the gym. on our shoulders, Miss Marie O'Toole."

"The bother of what?" demanded Marie blandly.

The freshman president explained, and Marie thanked her effusively for her trouble. "It's terrible not knowing any of these American college customs," she sighed. "But I'm learning pretty fast. I won't eat very much between now and the game, so in case you do have to carry me ——"

"Before we plan on that," put in the practical freshman, "we'd better go and get the mascots engaged and their clothes fixed up. It's going to be some work, I can tell you."

Whereat the deputation departed hastily in search of black Mandy and little Jim, of purple streamers, metal dish-cloths to serve as chain armor for the champion mascot, and canton flannel for the manufacture of a whole family of white rabbits—the white rabbit being the freshman class animal.

After that, rumors grew wilder and flew faster than ever, but none of them could be verified. The deputation, being composed of the most canny members of a large and brilliant class, shrouded all its proceedings in the deepest mystery; and Montana Marie's ideas about the scheme she was supposed to have devised were much too vague for expression. Having been ridiculed for her ignorance of college customs early in the fall term, Marie had speedily discovered that silence kept one from being laughed at. That it also gave one a reputation for diplomacy, for expert bluffing, and for wonderful eleventh hour inspirations, was a matter of small concern to Montana Marie, who had none of Straight Dutton's analytical interest in the queer crooks and turns of human nature.

The day of the great game found Harding

in a state of unparalleled excitement. There was the regular great-game-excitement and the special mystery-excitement. Could the freshmen possibly win? And how would they try to do it? The line in front of the gym. doors was of record length. Even Mariana Ellison, blasé C. P., who had never before let a mere game interfere with the unfolding of her literary emotions, was to be found in the ranks. Montana Marie was an usher. In a ravishing white gown, with a huge purple bow on her lovely hair and a purple wand in her hand, she helped to direct the surging freshman mob to its proper place in the purple-draped balcony. Arrangements in the freshman gallery seemed to be complicated. Ushers ran wildly to and fro. The song leader moved her box three times in response to their whispered instructions. Everybody else moved countless times. Choice seats were abandoned cheerfully for no obvious reason. An overdose of purple drapery obstructed the view at the center of the gallery, but nobody touched a single fold of the offending decoration.

"The quiet, well-mannered little dears!"

HE WAVED HIS PURPLE BANNER

jeered Fluffy Dutton from the riotous sophomore gallery. " I wonder if they'll wake up and take notice when their famous trick-play comes on the scene—and doesn't work ! "

But first the teams came on the scene, the Invincibles dancing gaily around little black Mandy, who was resplendent in a trailing red academic gown, with a small red mortar-board topping her fuzzy black braids. Little Mandy looked frightened and sucked her thumb, whereas Johnny Hawkins, in metal-dish-cloth and silver-paper armor, marched proudly at the head of the freshman players, and he waved his purple banner with its white rabbit emblem in a bold and fearless manner that quite upset the decorum of the purple gallery. But only for a moment ; the shrieks of delight were smothered before they were well begun ; songs were sung, not shouted ; clapping was subdued to a ladylike volume. Miss Andrews smiled approval at the purple gallery, whereat the leading spirits ensconced there winked joyously at one another. The plot was auspiciously launched.

For perhaps three minutes after Miss Andrews whistled the signal to the teams to

"Play ball," nothing particular happened. The freshman center muffed outrageously, the sophomore home barely missed making a goal, and the freshman guards seized the opportunity thus offered to do some very creditable interfering, which the center's stage-fright rendered quite useless. The ball was back at the sophomore basket, and the Invincible home had poised it again for an easy toss. Then there was a faint rustle in the purple gallery, then a breathless "Ah!" of amazement from the red one, followed by a suppressed titter of amusement. The Invincible home caught a hint of something in the air, hesitated, tossed up the ball, and missed the basket. In the mêlée that followed every member of the Invincibles took a second off to look around, and the freshmen scored. Whereupon black Mandy's Jim, whose striking costume of white and purple stripes had made his sudden appearance on the top rail of the purple gallery all the more spectacular, dropped back out of sight, before Miss Andrews had as much as discovered his presence. Annoyance and uncertainty as to what might happen next beset the Invincibles. The freshmen scored again. The purple gallery sang a polite song of triumph, then sat back behind the purple drapery and let the Invincibles score twice. Just as the most uncertain of the Invincible homes was about to score an inevitable point, standing close under the basket, something happened again. The voluminous purple drapery straightened out taut, disclosing itself as a huge purple banner with the class numerals on it in white; and at regular intervals on the white figures there were oval openings through which purple-capped faces popped out, grinning placidly across at the agitated red gallery. There was another rustle, a flutter, a giggle. The uncertain home missed her sure throw, there was a long, futile scramble for the ball, and Miss Andrews' silver whistle sounded the end of the half. Score two to two.

Instantly the purple gallery broke out in tuneful song, the sophomores in angry clamor. An indignant sophomore deputation beset Miss Andrews. The senior coaches came running out to join it. The junior coaches smilingly disclaimed all knowledge of the freshman plot to rattle the Invincibles. Miss Andrews had seen nothing; upon being enlightened she summoned the freshman president, who was also the leader of their music.

"But we aren't breaking any rule," that budding diplomatist explained politely. "We haven't shrieked or clapped noisily,—or stamped"—with a meaning glance at the sophomore delegation, who blushed at the veiled accusation. "Basket-ball is supposed to teach self-control, isn't it, Miss Andrews? The Invincibles oughtn't to pay any attention to sophomore giggles. Of course if it is against the rules to show extra-mascots —— But the sophomores shouted fearfully at first. That was what rattled our center so."

In the end the freshman president returned in triumph to the purple gallery, where immediately the purple banner was again spread out to while away the tedium of the intermission.

"You're smart, if you are mean," Fluffy Dutton called across the big gym. admiringly.

"Wait till you see the rest of our stunts," Montana Marie's clear voice sang back. "I guess you'll think we're smart before we're through. Well, rather!"

"Might as well enjoy whatever is doing,"

Fluffy advised her irate neighbors. "This whole business just shows that they knew they couldn't possibly win in a straight game. But it's awfully clever."

The Invincible team had arrived at the same philosophical conclusion. When they came back they bowed mockingly to the purple gallery, and cheered, in pantomime, below the mystic purple banner. They won a goal in spite of the disconcerting appearance on the freshman railing of a tiny yellow-haired child dressed as a purple Queen of Hearts. But when a whole family of white rabbits popped out at once, in assorted sizes, across the length of the purple gallery, they resigned themselves good-naturedly to the loss of not one goal only but two. When the banner unfurled again, this time with rabbit heads in the oval spaces, the prize center of the Invincibles happened to be facing it, and, being already half hysterical with weariness, she crumpled up with mirth. Before her sub. could trot out to the center field, the whistle had sounded the end of the great game. Score five to four in the freshmen's favor, fouls accounting for the extra points.

"Do the stunts all over again and maybe we'll forgive you," Fluffy sang across to the purple gallery. After the mascots had appeared once more, amid much applause, there was a rush for the gym. floor.

The players were all carried round the gym. on their partisans' shoulders, and Montana Marie O'Toole, smiling as serenely as though it were an every-day occurrence, also got her promised ride.

As she was let carefully down to the floor again, she found herself face to face with Straight Dutton.

"I say," began Straight, "did you think of all that nonsense?"

Marie flashed her a knowing smile. "You're too flattering, Miss Dutton, I assure you," she parried.

"Not at all," said Straight with asperity. "I think the whole performance was extra-specially silly. It just spoiled the game. You've won technically, of course, but not by playing ball."

Montana Marie thrust her smiling face, topped by the huge purple bow, close to Straight's flushed, tired one. "Don't you tell a soul, and I'll tell you a secret," she whispered impressively.

"Cross my heart," promised Straight eagerly.

"Well, then, I'm sorry you lost," whispered Montana Marie. "All my best friends are seniors, and I hate to see them looking so blue. Now don't you tell!" Montana Marie joined a band of dancing freshmen and was whisked off down the gym.

Straight looked after her half admiringly, half angrily. "Just the same I don't believe she thought it up. She's the best bluffer that ever came to Harding. Smile, look mysterious, say nothing—that's her trick-play, and it always scores. I wonder why she was so crazy to come to Harding. I certainly must ask Betty if she ever has wondered why her freshman was so stuck on Harding College."

Then, as her twin rushed up with a reminder that it was time to dress for the team dinner, "Yes, Fluffy," Straight answered absently, "I'm coming this very minute. But I certainly should like to know—nothing you can tell me, Fluff; so don't ask me to stop and explain."

CHAPTER XIII

MONTANA MARIE had dozens of invitations
to spend the spring vacation with college
friends. But she declined them all. " You
see, Ma misses me a lot," she explained, " and
she's been counting on coming East to help
me buy my spring clothes. So I guess I can't
very well disappoint her."

So Mrs. and Miss O'Toole became for a
week leading features of New York's largest
and showiest hotel; and there various of
Marie's New York friends, encountering the
pair in the corridors or the tea-room, or dining wonderfully behind a screen of hovering
waiters, were treated to samples of Mrs.
O'Toole's choice observations, couched in Mrs.
O'Toole's choice English. Sometimes Marie
giggled amiably at her mother's remarks, and
sometimes she explained " what Ma really
means to say." But she never appeared em-

212

barrassed, never showed annoyance, and never though invitations were again showered upon her, accepted one that did not include Mrs. O'Toole.

"You see Ma's been expecting a good time this week," she explained simply. "She's come way from California to see me, and so I guess I can't leave her alone much."

And for every girl who made fun of Mrs. O'Toole, there was another to defend Marie's loyalty; so that she went back for her spring term at Harding more talked about than ever, more laughed at, and more stoutly championed.

Having discovered the rules of true concentration, Marie had plenty of time for recreation, especially now that soft April breezes had melted hard faculty hearts, and spring-term standards made life easy. She entered into all the season's diversions with her customary zest, but the event that fairly stirred her soul was the junior prom. For one day —nay, two,—the Harding campus would be black with men! Montana Marie sighed joyously at this pleasing prospect, and listened eagerly to the plans, hopes, fears, and disappointments that preluded the great occasion.

Connie wasn't going to the prom., Montana Marie discovered to her horror. The idea of missing your junior prom. !

"Why aren't you going?" she demanded incisively.

"Because I don't know any man to ask," Connie replied with her usual directness.

"Goodness!" sighed Montana Marie. "Why, I know dozens of men! I'll get you a man, and you can save me one little dance in exchange for him. Do you prefer that Winsted senior that Mr. Ford brought to call on me last week—you saw him in the parlor when you came down to dinner, so you can size him up—or would you rather have a man that I met when I was in New York? They won't want to go with you? Nonsense! Any man wants to go to a Harding prom. Give me two dances, if it will make you feel any better about it."

Connie's good fortune having been noised abroad, Georgia Ames made prompt application for a man.

"They always let in a few seniors, you know,

and I'm pining to be one of them. Ask the New York man for me, and you can have three perfectly good dances as your reward."

"Done!" giggled Montana Marie joyously. "Say, if I provided men for enough juniors and seniors, why, I could get a whole program of dances for myself, couldn't I? I'm just longing for a real man-dance. I went to one in New York, and it just started me up. Georgia, tell your nice junior friends about me, won't you? There's a man in Chicago that could come to this prom. as well as not, and a man at Yale, and two in Malden, Mass., and—oh, well, just dozens of them. I've got letters from most of them here. The girls can read the letters and take their pick. Why, this prom.'s going to be real exciting, if I am only a little freshman that's supposed to sit on the fire-escape and watch the fun. You're sure there won't be any trouble about smuggling me in?"

Georgia was confident that there would not be any trouble on that score. "You can be a freshman waitress," she explained. "You would be anyway, because they always pick out the prettiest ones to serve the lemonade.

And then you can just abandon the lemonade, and dance. It's been done before now, I guess."

Montana Marie smiled engagingly. "If I got an extra man for myself, why, then you poor things wouldn't have to sit out the dances that you gave me."

Georgia shook her head doubtfully at that suggestion. "You'd better not try it. It's rather nice for us to sit out—gives us a chance to cool off in peace now and then. Anyway, freshman waitresses aren't supposed to ask men for themselves. You couldn't do it."

"All right," agreed Montana Marie complacently. "I don't want to do anything that isn't done. Georgia, how would you like a Montana cowboy for your prom. man?"

"Depends on how well he can dance," Georgia parried.

"Oh, he can dance all right enough," Montana Marie assured her. "There's only one trouble ——"

"Of course," laughed Georgia. "The trouble that's common to all the nicest prom. men. They can't come."

"Oh, he'd come fast enough, if I asked

him," Montana Marie declared easily. "He'd come like lightning. But when he got here I'm afraid he'd want at least six dances with me. And that's too much for any junior to give up. So, as I can't have an extra man for myself, I can't ask him."

"Too bad," sympathized Georgia. "I'll go and tell some juniors about your Prom. Man Supply Company. Are you sure the men's letters can be on exhibition?"

"Oh, yes," agreed Montana Marie carelessly. "You see, I used to like some of those men pretty well once on a time, but now —— Oh, yes, they can choose by the letters if they want to."

As a matter of fact, no patron of the Prom. Man Supply Company made use of the proprietor's private correspondence in making her choice from the "dozens" of available prom. men. They all left the question of suitability to Marie, who discussed qualifications at length with her patrons, considered each case with the same care that she bestowed on the intricacies of Latin prose, and sent off her invitations-by-proxy with a confidence that was the admiration of all beholders. But her proverbial good luck held. All the men that she asked promptly accepted; and to a woman did each patron find satisfaction in her allotment. The fee per man was necessarily reduced to two dances, and counting in the one dance promised to Jim Watson, who had written to announce that he was coming up to help Betty chaperon the party, Marie's program was full, except for supper and the last dance; and Marie was the envy of her class, and more of a celebrity than ever.

And then Marie was late for the first dance. It had been such hard work introducing everybody and arranging things, she explained glibly, when she finally hurried in just in time for one short turn around the hall with Connie's man from Winsted. She was wearing a black and white dress, with touches of vivid scarlet.

"I guess you'll find me all right for our next dance," she told the Winsted man gaily. "You'd know this dress as far as you can see it. That's always one good thing about the clothes Ma picks out for me."

Then came Jim's dance. Montana Marie sweetly begged Betty to keep it for herself, but when Betty laughingly declared that Jim had made that waltz a condition of coming up for the prom., she swept him off across the still empty floor. Betty watched her vivid gown weaving in and out in the crowd, as couple after couple joined the dance, and then lost sight of her, and forgot all about her, until first Georgia, then Timmy Wentworth, and next Connie, each followed by a dejected-looking escort, came to ask if she had seen anything of Montana Marie.

At the end of the second dance, it seemed, Montana Marie O'Toole had vanished magically from the junior prom. The men who had gathered from near and far to bask in her smiles, as their reward for doing escort duty to her friends, departed with only one last tantalizing glimpse of her. This they got when she reappeared just in time to dance the last waltz. She danced it with a man who had not been invited to the prom. for any patroness of the Prom. Man Supply Company. And just before the music stopped she vanished once more, not to reappear until the following morning, when she achieved the masterly feat of taking six men to chapel, and three others to breakfast afterward at the Tally-ho, with complete satisfaction to all parties concerned. It remained only to pacify the patronesses of the Prom. Man Supply Company, and to them she made full and unabashed explanation of her conduct.

"I don't wonder you thought I was perfectly outrageous, if you didn't get any of my messages. Why, I sent dozens of messages to all of you! You see I felt horribly sick and dizzy after the second dance—I thought of course Mr. Watson noticed it. So I went out to get some air. I came back after a while, but the lights and the heat made me dreadfully giddy again. So off I dashed. But I did hate to miss everything, so I slipped in for the last waltz. That man —oh, he wasn't one of the Prom. Man Supply ones. He was— well, you pick out the most unselfish junior you can think of,—one who'd be capable of giving up her last beautiful prom. waltz to a poor unfortunate little freshman,—and maybe you'll guess right."

"Did you have a good supper?" asked Timmy Wentworth abruptly. She had heard strange rumors of a waiter's having been exorbitantly tipped by a couple who had bribed him to bring their supper down to the apple orchard.

Montana Marie laughed delightedly. "How did you know about that?" she demanded. "I didn't eat any dinner because I'd been to so many prom. teas in the afternoon; but when I began to feel queer in the evening, I thought perhaps a cup of coffee and a sandwich would do me good. So I got a nice waiter to bring me some outside. Wasn't that all right? Weren't there coffee and sandwiches enough to go round?"

Timmy nodded, smiling a sarcastic little smile. "Plenty, thank you. Was the man in the hammock, who helped you get and eat the sandwich, also lent by that same very accommodating junior?"

Montana Marie stared in offended dignity. "Wouldn't almost any junior, especially those that I'd asked men for, be pleased to lend me a man to find a waiter and then show him where I was sitting out in the orchard—feeling quite ill and giddy?" Montana Marie's tone changed suddenly, growing soft and persuasive. "Say, I almost forgot to tell you what George Dorsey said about you. He said that you were just exactly his ideal of an American college girl, and he hopes to come up here again next month."

Timmy Wentworth smiled—this time cordially. For she had found George Dorsey a very satisfactory example of the American college man. "He said something to me about motoring up in June," she admitted, "and I hope he will. He's very nice, if he is an arrant flatterer. I'm really ever so much obliged to you, Marie, for asking him up for me. Come to dinner to-night, and I'll tell you all the jists that happened."

"I'm not going to bother her any more about how she spent her evening," Timmy told Georgia later. "It was slightly embarrassing for a few minutes, consoling poor Mr. Dorsey for the loss of the only two dances that he specially wanted. But that's over and done with now, and the way she acted is her own affair."

"I hate a person who cuts dances," declared honest Georgia bluntly.

"Maybe she did really feel ill."

"She seems to have felt like flirting around

in the moonlight. Eugenia Ford saw her holding hands on the Morton steps."

" With the same mysterious man?"

" Eugenia couldn't be sure."

" Whose was he, I wonder? He was nothing so much of a dancer."

" He looked nice and big and brown and jolly."

" And he never took his eyes off Marie once. That was the principal thing I noticed about him."

Timmy's generous attitude toward the manager of the Prom. Man Supply Company was promptly adopted by the other patronesses. So easily placated, indeed, and so agreeable were they, that Montana Marie, who had basely deceived them with half truths and timely repetitions of vain compliments, was speedily stricken with remorse. A few days after the prom. she sought out Betty, and told her all about it.

" You see, Miss Wales, I did feel ill. I'd worried so about all those men, and I'd talked so hard all the afternoon. And then a man from home came to see me—somebody I know awfully well. Of course he wanted to come

to the prom., but Georgia had said I couldn't
have anybody, so—well, I couldn't be rude
and leave him. I just told him I didn't care
about the prom. You see, Miss Wales, even
if I'd smuggled him in, I hadn't any dances
left for him—but two. And that isn't his
idea of going to a dance with me. So we just
wandered around in the cool, and Fred got a
waiter to bring us elegant things to eat, and
when the last dance came we just calmly
walked in—all the ushers and doorkeepers
had gone away by that time. We simply
couldn't resist that music. And I've let them
suppose, Miss Wales,—I've pretty nearly said
to those other girls that I cut dances with,—
that some junior gave up her last dance and
her man to me. Do you think that was perfectly horrid of me, Miss Wales?"

" Of course I think it's always better to tell
things just as they are." Betty tried to be
tactful and truthful at once.

Marie nodded vigorous agreement. " I
should say it is. You get all tangled up and
ashamed of yourself when you try to fix up a
good story. You see, Miss Wales, I wrote
Fred about the prom., and about the men I'd

asked for those juniors, and he just up and came himself. I didn't ask him. I especially explained that I couldn't ask any one for myself. But he was bound to come along just the same."

" Rather a long trip, wasn't it?" asked Betty, feeling her way a little.

"Oh, well, he's going to stay East quite a while, I guess," Marie told her.

And then for no reason at all Marie blushed furiously, laughed at herself for blushing, and finally explained that Fred had never been 'way East before and it made her laugh to remember the comical things he had told about his long journey. " He's in New York now," she went on. " I expect he's doing the town in real cowboy and miner style. He's a sure enough cowboy and miner, Miss Wales."

" Is he coming up here again?" asked Betty, just to show an interest.

"Oh, I don't know," said Montana Marie gaily. Then she flushed and laughed again. " If you want my honest opinion, I should say that he very likely is. Now I'll go and make myself square with Georgia and Miss Wentworth and the rest of them. They are awfully

easy marks, or they'd have seen through me.
Good-bye, Miss Wales. No warnings so far,
and concentration is working to the queen's
taste."

CHAPTER XIV

ENTERTAINING GEORGIA'S SISTER

GEORGIA AMES was blue about something. As the spring term wore on toward June she grew absent and pensive to a marked degree. It wasn't that she was a senior; Georgia Ames wasn't the sort to mope because college was almost over for her. Besides, she and Lucile Merrifield and the Dutton twins were going to Lucile's camp in the Maine woods for a long, blissful summer. That certainly wasn't a prospect to make you dread the plunge into the wide, wide world. It was only the girls who didn't know what was coming next, or who knew and didn't like it, who moped through their last spring term.

The Duttons were pathetically worried about Georgia's low spirits. Straight suggested a doctor; Fluffy adroitly sounded Georgia on the subject of conditions, and discussed the ethics of " flunking out " seniors exhaustively, until Georgia suggested mildly that the subject wasn't of any great interest to her.

227

"I'm thankful to say I've never had to worry about flunking," she said, "and none of our crowd has either—oh, I forgot Eugenia Ford when she was a freshman. But that was pure silliness."

So the matter of conditions was definitely eliminated.

"Maybe she's in love," suggested Montana Marie, who was present one day when the subject was discussed. "Being in love makes you feel—well, queer. And if it's not returned ——"

"What a little goose you are, Marie, on the subject of men," Timmy Wentworth told her shortly. "No sensible girl like G. Ames goes around wearing her heart on her sleeve. Besides, Georgia doesn't care for men at all. She often says that she came to college in the first place because there wouldn't be any men around."

"She did!" sighed Montana Marie. "What a queer reason! I ——"

"Oh, yes, do tell us why you came," Straight Dutton broke in, as Marie hesitated.

"Why I came?" repeated Marie gaily. "Oh, yes, I'll tell you that with pleasure. I

came to complete my education, of course."
When Straight gave a disappointed little
shrug, Marie giggled riotously. "Sorry you
don't like my reason," she concluded, drawing
down the corners of her pretty mouth in an
absurd imitation of extreme grief.

It was little Binks Ames, with her queer
talent for making strange discoveries, who
finally found out what was worrying Georgia.
And she took the matter to the most wonderful person about troubles that she knew:
namely, Miss Betty Wales.

"You see," said Binks solemnly, "Constance
Ames is the pretty, society kind of girl. But
she's awfully bright, too. She's five years
younger than Georgia; so she'll be a year
younger in entering college. That is, if she
will come, when she's ready, in the fall. But
she won't. She has an idea that college is
awfully solemn and serious and studious, and
she says she'd rather go to boarding-school,
where the girls are lively, even if there are a
lot of rules. And Georgia feels dreadfully.
She's always thought it would be such fun
having Constance here after she's graduated."

"You'll be here, anyway," laughed Betty.

"Oh, but I don't count," little Binks explained quite seriously. "At least not like a younger sister that you can come up with in September, and send boxes to, and introduce to your friends, and talk it all over with in vacations. Besides, I'm—I'm queer. So I don't really count at all."

"I see." Betty was as serious as Binks. "Why doesn't Georgia have her little sister up here for a visit? She'd be sure to have a splendid time, and then she'd want to enter college. Has she put in her application for the campus?"

Binks nodded. "Georgia did it for her the minute she saw how nice Harding is. The reason Georgia doesn't have her up is because she's afraid to. You see, Constance belongs to a crowd of boys and girls who have a lot going on all the time, and Georgia is afraid—well, to tell the truth, Constance is man-crazy. She doesn't think you can have a good time with just girls. And of course when you don't expect a good time and act offish and disagreeable, why, you don't have a good time," ended Binks acutely.

Betty nodded. "And Georgia is afraid Constance would feel and act that way if she came for the visit. She might, of course. I don't quite see what I can do about it, but I'll think. I certainly ought to come to Georgia's rescue once, when she's always coming to mine."

"She was just awfully proud of being elected Georgia-to-the-Rescue," confided Binks. "She said she was as proud of that as of being taken into Dramatic Club."

"Really?" Betty flushed with pleasure. "What a foolish, sweet way to feel about just helping me! Well, I'll think hard about the man-struck Constance. We'll both think hard, and perhaps we can think of a way to rescue Georgia."

"Oh, I'm sure you can," said Binks with touching confidence. "The thing to do is to make Constance expect a good time, isn't it, Miss Wales? Because then she couldn't help liking Harding, especially in spring term."

Yes, that was clearly the thing to do, Betty agreed, and Binks, remembering suddenly that Miss Wales was very busy and quite capable of making her own deductions about what to do in regard to Constance, took a blushing departure.

That same afternoon the B. C. A.'s gathered informally in the top story of the Peter Pan annex ; and when the matter of Georgia's blues came up, Betty told them in confidence what Binks had discovered.

" Whatever is done will have to be done right away," she added, " because campus rooms are assigned early in June, and when Constance gets hers I suppose she will give it up. If she should change her mind later about coming to college, she couldn't get back her chance at the room. She would have to apply all over again, and that means that she wouldn't be on the campus before her senior year, if she was then."

" Foolish young Constance ! " said Mary scornfully. " The idea of thinking that Harding girls are less fun than boarding-school chits."

" The idea of thinking that there isn't time enough later on for men," sniffed Babbie, playing with her engagement ring.

" The idea of thinking that she won't change her mind about men and most other things, while she's here," added little Helen Adams, with a comical air of vast experience.

"Georgia ought to be game and take the risk of having foolish young Constance up for a week," declared Christy Mason. " We'd get her so properly excited that she'd forget the name of her best particular suitor."

Madeline listened to these comments with an air of polite detachment. Finally she rose from her place and crawled over Betty to the Peter Pan staircase. " Talk about something else until I get back," she ordered. " I'm going down to the Tally-ho desk to write a letter for Georgia to send to Constance."

It was fully twenty minutes before Madeline reappeared, waving the letter in her hand. " Want to hear it? " she asked. " It's nothing much, but I'm pretty sure it will get young Constance. Listen now, and don't ask questions, because I won't answer.

" DEAR CONSTANCE :
        " Can't you come up next Thursday for a week ? I shall be rather busy then—seniors are terribly busy in spring term (having a good time)—but Billy Barstow is to be here that week, and is crazy to meet you and show you the place. Timmy Wentworth wants to take you canoeing. Dickie Drake is coming

up to see a sister or a cousin or something, and you two can go buggy-riding mornings, while cousin and I are at classes. (Of course you know you're not allowed to go buggy-riding with a man after you enter.) You're also invited to a fraternity dance at Winsted,—not particularly exciting; so perhaps, unless you're coming up next year and want to meet some Winsted men, it wouldn't pay you to go. Let me know whether to accept for you.

" But at all events, don't fail to come up.

" GEORGIA.

" P. S.—Of course all my friends are planning to do things for you. Don't let them know that girls bore you, because it would hurt their feelings so."

Madeline folded the letter carefully and tucked it up her sleeve for safe-keeping. " Rather nice on the whole, isn't it ? " she said. " It does just what Binks astutely pointed out must be done. It brings young Constance to Harding in an expectant and receptive frame of mind."

" She may be angry when she finds she's been fooled," suggested Christy.

Madeline stared at her blankly. " You don't really mean," she began at last, " that

you doubt the combined ability of the B. C.
A.'s, Timmy Wentworth, Dickie Drake, Billy
Barstow, the Dutton twins, and the best frat.
in Winsted to give foolish young Constance
the time of her gay young life? If she is any
kind of a girl she will think we're the very
best jokers she ever heard of. The Duttons
are down in the Tally-ho waiting to carry the
letter to Georgia, and if she likes the idea
they're going to take charge of the program—
select entertainers, assign stunts and hours,
and all that. Eugenia Ford is going to attend to the Winsted end. There's no fooling
about that dance, Christy. It's the most
gorgeous affair of the Winsted season, Eugenia
says, and she is sure she can get an invitation
for Constance. Any more objections?"

There were no more objections. As the full
beauty of Madeline's plan dawned upon the
other B. C. A.'s, there were shrieks of delight,
offers of assistance, and suggestions for novel
stunts likely to appeal particularly to the
temperament of foolish young Constance.
Presently the Duttons trilled from below, and
the letter was ceremoniously lowered in the
Peter Pan basket, amid great excitement.

" We forgot Bob Blake," Straight called up. "She'll be splendid to help."

" All right, but don't alter the letter. We can mention her at the station," Madeline called down ; and the twins and Eugenia hurried off to the Belden to find Georgia.

It was on the loveliest of May afternoons, a week later, that Constance Ames alighted with much youthful dignity from the Boston train, to find herself fairly surrounded by a noisy bevy of girls,—girls quite as pretty and quite as stylish as young Constance, girls whose flattering speeches of welcome made her blush, whose jokes made her laugh, and whose breezy energy packed her and her bag, together with six or seven of themselves, into a trim runabout and rushed her off to the Tally-ho for refreshment, before she had had time to explain that she was hot and dusty and would rather go straight to her room,—before she met any more girls or any men.

The Tally-ho was so fascinating and the food so good that Constance decided not to say anything about leaving in a hurry. And then all at once the Dutton twins, whom chemistry lab. had prevented from meeting Constance at the station, burst upon the scene.

" Eugenia Ford has a car up for the rest of the term—a big snorting red one, with a rumbly horn and a funny French chauffeur. She wants any ten of us to go riding in it, in honor of Georgia's sister."

" How do you do, Georgia's sister ? " added Straight gravely. " Awfully nice to have you here to give parties for. Eugenia has an extra veil in the car for you. She says for everybody to leave their hats here, to save room."

" We'll have eats at Mossy Glen."

" Who's seen to the food ? "

" Over the Notch by moonlight and home through Winsted, to let John Ford see his little cousin splurge. She's telephoned him to be on the watch for us."

" Timmy Wentworth can't get away this evening to go canoeing, so Eugenia's party just fits in."

" Wouldn't Miss Constance Ames like a wash and a brush in Betty's private dressing room ? She looks extra-specially spick and span, but traveling in the heat always makes a person feel messy."

Constance went off with Betty and Madeline, and Georgia went out to break the news to Eugenia that Constance generally took hours and hours to prink up. To her amazement and relief Constance appeared within five minutes.

During the ride there were frequent, though vague, references to Timmy and Dick and Billy. Everybody in the party seemed to know and like them, and they seemed to have planned all sorts of delightful entertainment for Constance. Timmy, Fluffy Dutton declared solemnly, would be simply heart-broken at having to postpone the canoeing trip on Paradise, which had been planned for the first evening of Constance's visit.

" I'm having a beautiful time, all the same," Constance assured Fluffy eagerly. " I just love motoring. And I'm very anxious to see Winsted."

But a bad puncture, necessitating a long delay, put the détour to Winsted out of the evening's program. How much Madeline's firm determination that Winsted should be kept for the dessert of Constance's visit, as it were, had to do with the French chauffeur's deliberation in repairing the puncture, is a matter for idle speculation.

Next morning Constance was awakened with a start by a huge bunch of wild forget-me-nots, which hurtled in at her window, and plopped down beside her on the bed.

" How lovely ! " murmured Constance, burying her face in the big blue bouquet. " And a note hidden in them ! What fun ! Just like a story."

The note was from Timmy Wentworth. " Your sister is busy all this morning. She says you are to take breakfast at nine at Cuyler's with the Misses Dutton. They will call for you. At ten won't you meet me at the boat-house for our paddle ? It will give me such pleasure. Timmy Wentworth."

Constance dressed with eager haste. The Duttons were in their liveliest mood. Cuyler's waffles fairly melted in your mouth. And at ten she was going canoeing with Timmy Wentworth !

The Duttons escorted her as far as the top of Observatory Hill, and having pointed out the boat-house, departed unceremoniously for a ten o'clock quiz. Constance consulted a tiny mirror that hung from her silver chain, smoothed her hair, straightened her coat collar, and walked leisurely down, through the campus gardens and past the famous frog pond, to Paradise. At the top of the boat-house stairs she paused and looked to see if Timmy was waiting. It was too dark inside the boat-house to see any one, but on the railing perched a tall, merry-faced girl in a blue and white jumper, who waved friendly greetings. She must have been one of the crowd at the station, Constance reflected, and she waved back cordially as she hurried down the stairs.

" Lovely day, isn't it? " The tall girl's firm hand-shake made Constance wince. " And the woods are full of flowers. Fluffy and I were out before breakfast getting a boatful for the Belden House senior tea. We stole out a bunch for you. Shall we be off? "

" Ye-es," stammered Constance. " That is, I was expecting —— "

" How stupid! " broke in the tall girl eagerly. " I forgot to say that I'm Felicia

A TALL, MERRY-FACED GIRL

Wentworth, commonly known as Timmy for no reason under the sun. Now shall we be off?"

"Oh, yes," said Constance hastily, too proud to show either astonishment or disappointment. It was an entertaining trip, too, in spite of everything. Timmy was not at all Constance's idea of a college grind. She had just come back from a Dartmouth prom. She was going home next Saturday to see about her junior usher dress, and incidentally to star in an amateur vaudeville performance at the Country Club her family belonged to. It appeared that amateur vaudeville shows, tennis, canoeing, and going to "stunty" house-parties—she was going to "a duck of a one" in June—were Timmy's chief diversions. Yet she confided to Constance that she was hoping hard to make the Phi Kappa honor list next year, and that she had spent the previous afternoon in "digging fiercely" on a philosophy paper, because "if you had a good head for books what was the use of muddling along?"

"The fun here is in pulling off the work and still getting in the fun," she assured Constance, paddling up a tiny bay, whose banks were blue with forget-me-nots. Timmy dropped her paddle, brushed the hair out of her eyes, and smiled engagingly at young Constance. "You understand what I mean, of course," she flattered adroitly. "I can see that you're not the muddling kind. Anyway Georgia says you are very clever. Well, all I say is, look at me and don't worry about the good times we have. Now shall we get the Belden a little more forget-me-not for its sentimental senior party?"

Constance spoke enthusiastically to Georgia of Paradise and Miss Wentworth. She dropped not a hint of surprises or disappointments. That afternoon Billy Barstow, a petite, pretty sophomore, with a distinctly frivolous air, took Constance for a stroll round the campus. It was hot, and they spent most of the time in the gym. basement, watching the divers in the swimming-tank and exchanging confidences about many things. Billy was secretly bored, but she concealed it so well that Constance decided Billy should be her first crush. Billy had put this idea into her head by explaining how Georgia had been her first crush. Dickie Drake appeared a day or two later. She wasn't pretty, but she was very distinguished-looking, Constance decided. She was also engaged, and willing to talk about Tom to anybody who would listen,—even to Georgia's sub-freshman sister.

"She'll get her self-consciousness knocked out of her in short order up here," Dick assured the cousin whom she had come to visit. "And then she'll be a very nice child. Remember what a detestable little prig I was when I came up—a snob and man-crazy and insufferably lazy. And they turned me out a rather decent sort—not half good enough for Tom, but much improved."

Everybody agreed that young Constance showed the proper spirt in ignoring the base deception that had been practiced upon her, and in appearing to enjoy every minute of her week in Harding. Even the stony-hearted Madeline admitted that she had richly earned her Winsted dessert. And so the most select frat. in Winsted found its end-of-the-season dance mysteriously turned into an ovation for a pretty sub-freshman friend of Eugenia

Ford's. As the sub-freshman was undeniably a "winner," the frat. forgave John Ford for making such a fuss about her, and promptly added her name to the next year's guest-list. Which meant that foolish young Constance would not pine away for lack of masculine society, if she decided to enter Harding in the fall.

"It's queer about nicknames," said Straight Dutton, waving her handkerchief after Constance's Boston-bound train. "It's queer how many nicest girls get tagged with boys' names. Young Constance has confided to Georgia that she'll have a try at Harding. Now what got her was that Timmy and Dickie and Bill and Bob Blake are all the finest ever. If they hadn't been, everything would have gone to smash. It's certainly queer how many nicest girls get nicknamed Bob and Bill and Dickie."

"The reason," said Madeline wisely, "is that the very nicest girls are all-around nice— not sissy nice, or young-lady nice, or clever nice, but nice every way,—and just as good fun to play about with as any man in the world. And the rest of us notice that, with-

out stopping to analyze it, and call them Bob
or Billy."

"Um—maybe you're right," said Straight
slowly. "I presume you are. All I know
for sure is that we've scored. Hurray for
Billy and Bob and Dickie and Timmy!
Hurrah for we, us, and company that planned
it all! Hurray for Harding!"

CHAPTER XV

THE NEW WOMAN AT HARDING

" GOODNESS! I'm glad I elected this sociology course." Fluffy Dutton precipitated herself through the half-open door of Timmy Wentworth's big corner double (universally called Timmy's room, though half of it, of course, belonged to Sallie Wright), tossed her note-book on the table, dexterously extracted two fat cushions from behind Eugenia Ford's head, and as dexterously inserted them and herself on Sallie's couch, in a practically invisible vacancy between Straight and Montana Marie O'Toole. There were plenty of other seats to choose from, but Fluffy was intent on securing a central position as regards both the conversation and the refreshments which her keen eyes had detected in Susanna Hart's lap.

There were loud remonstrances from Eugenia and Straight, amused giggles from Montana Marie, and then, because it was a hot, unprofitable May day, with " absolutely nothing doing," as Straight had just remarked, objections to Fluffy's high-handed conduct subsided in favor of an interest in Fluffy's sudden and amazing fondness for sociology.

"But you've said right along that you hated it because it came in the afternoon," Eugenia reminded her.

"And because of all the reference reading," added Straight.

"And the awful way Miss Seaton does her hair," put in Montana Marie, with another giggle.

"Frivolous objections, all of them." Fluffy reached a long arm for the candy. "Miss Seaton is a fright, and the library ought to buy more books and save us the nerve-racking scramble for them. And it's a burning shame to put a course as important as this one at such an absurd hour. But just the same"—Fluffy's manner took on the patronizing air of the over-indulged, because soon-departing senior—"just the same I advise all you juniors and sophs, and you, Montana Marie, if you ever should get to be a senior, to elect sociology and find out a few things about this woman question."

"This woman question!" repeated Susanna Hart scornfully. "Do you mean equal suffrage and all sorts of other boring subjects like that?"

Fluffy waited to finish a large mouthful. "Suffrage isn't a bore. It's a matter that every intelligent woman ought to think about at least."

"Don't quote Celissa Seaton, Fluffy," Straight told her severely. "Her style of oratory doesn't suit you at all. No matter how long you live, nor how frightfully you get to doing up your back hair, you'll never pass for the intellectual woman type, I'm happy to say."

"There you are again!" objected Fluffy eagerly. "Mixing up pretty clothes and a talent for making smooth and becoming puffs with baby-doll brains. Intelligent women nowadays aren't dowds, Straight."

"Some are. Example, Miss Celissa Seaton," retorted Straight promptly.

"Go it, twins." Montana Marie passed the candy to the combatants impartially, but Fluffy refused it and sat up with dignity against her stolen cushions.

"Honestly, girls, I'm serious about this sociology. When you're almost through college, you look back over the work you've had, and wish you could remember more about it, and are pretty sure that you'll remember a lot less before long, and anyway that a lot of it hasn't much to do with real life. Greek prose, for instance, and trig. and —syllogisms."

"I certainly hope I shan't encounter any syllogisms in real life," put in Straight fervently. "Because if I do, there's one thing certain ; they'll be sure to come out wrong and leave me in a fix."

"But you're glad of all the poetry you've learned to like," went on Fluffy, "and of the serious reading you've done and got off your mind for good. And the history and civil government will come in handy in polite conversation. But for real, downright, sit-up-and-take-notice interest, give me this sociology business. I tell you it sets a person thinking! If it didn't make me sort of faint to poke around in dirty, smelly places, I believe I should take up settlement work next winter. Lots of the girls in the class want to."

"Is sociology all about poor people?" inquired Timmy Wentworth. " Because I think myself that rich people are just exactly as interesting. Unless poor people are funny enough to make you laugh I think they're often very dull indeed. Consequently I don't believe settlement work is all fun and frolic."

" It's about both rich and poor people," explained Fluffy patiently. " But it hasn't anything much to do with their being bright or stupid. That comes in psych. mostly—people's minds. It's more about,—well, their all getting their rights, you know, and having a fair chance."

" Oh, yes, and the woman question means woman's rights, I suppose," piped up Susanna Hart, still scornfully.

" Well, you want your rights, don't you ?" Straight demanded, coming to Fluffy's rescue, as she always did the minute an outsider attacked her sister. " I never noticed you giving away bath hours or chances at library books, and your reputation as a freshman roommate ——" Straight paused and smiled meaningly around the circle. " No use rak-

ing up last year's scandal," she ended mildly,
perceiving from Susanna's flushed face that
she had scored.

" Well, but that's different, Straight," protested Susanna, humbled, but not ready to
yield her point. "Of course I take what's
coming to me. I certainly don't intend to lie
down and be walked over by—by anybody."
Susanna clenched her small hands wrathfully,
as she remembered the tyrannical last year's
roommate. "I didn't mean to be more
disagreeable about it than I had to, but I
want —— "

" Exactly," popped in Straight coolly.
" You want your rights."

" Well, I don't want to vote," snapped Susanna, " and I think suffragists are horrid
bores."

" How many do you know, Susanna?" inquired Fluffy sweetly.

" Celissa Seaton and—you," retorted Susanna. "Of course you're not a bore in general, Fluffy dear, but if you're going off on
that horrid subject —— "

" Well, of course I can't talk very interestingly about it," Fluffy conceded diplomatic-

ally. "I don't know enough to. But you should hear Miss Seaton. You'd have to find some other word besides bore to express your opinion of her, because you simply couldn't call her that. She gets all pink and excited, and she looks positively pretty in spite of her hair. Don't you know how Miss Ferris is always saying that everybody is interesting if you can only find the right thing to talk about? Well, Miss Seaton is just splendid on the woman question."

"And are you really a suffragist, Fluffy?" inquired Sallie Wright, in an awestruck voice. Not being at all clever herself, Sallie admired the Duttons from a safe distance, and spent hours pondering over their idiosyncrasies.

"Oh, not so you'd notice it," Fluffy told her. "Sorry to reduce the number of your suffragist friends to one, Susanna; but I'm still on the fence. I've chosen the anti-suffrage position for my final essay in the course, but so far, I may say, the arguments look to me pretty slim. If any idiotic man can vote, why in the world shouldn't we?"

"I thought Montana Marie's extra-special show settled all that foolishness," said Timmy

Wentworth. " It made fun of all those queer advanced notions, specially suffrage, and as far as I could see it did 'em up brown."

Fluffy sighed again patiently. " There you go again. It made fun ! You can make fun of anything—anything under the sun. But what have you proved ? What did that silly suffrage skit prove ? What did our ' Before Breakfast, Never After ' farce prove? Nothing ! " concluded Fluffy dramatically.

" Well, they were certainly oceans of fun," declared Sallie Wright feelingly.

" And apparently they did oceans of harm," Fluffy took her up, " if they gave you and Timmy and all your little pals the idea that nonsense like that is any real argument against the sensible modern ideas about women. Miss Seaton felt that way about the show, but I thought she was dippy. Now I'm almost sorry I went in for it."

" I believe Fluff's got a crush on Celissa Seaton," Straight called across Fluffy in a stage whisper directed at Montana Marie. Before Fluffy had time to retort, the door opened and Georgia Ames appeared.

" Oh, Georgia ! " Fluffy welcomed her with

enthusiasm. "Come and help me explain about sociology to these infants."

Georgia grinned cheerfully around the circle, dropped down Turk-fashion on the floor by the window, emptied the candy-box of its small remaining store, and complied in her usual effective fashion with Fluffy's request. "Celissa Seaton is certainly making a hit this term. I've just come from a wild sociological discussion on the shores of the swimming tank. We about decided to organize a College Woman's Rights Club. Let's do it right now, and get ahead of that other bunch."

"Splendid!" cried Susanna Hart traitorously. Susanna knew when she was beaten, and she had no desire to lead a lost cause against Georgia and the twins. "I just love to help organize things."

"So do I," agreed Montana Marie. "Only why not organize something a little more amusing, while we're about it? Eating is the feature of clubs that always appeals most to me."

"But there's no point in organizing anything amusing at this late date," Straight explained. "That is, not for us seniors."

" Besides, we've done plenty of that sort of thing before," added Georgia. " We've bequeathed any number of amusing organizations to Harding. Now we propose to bequeath something useful."

" And of course we depend on the rest of you to keep it going when we're gone," added Fluffy, smiling seductively at Susanna.

" All right," agreed the little sophomore.

" We're all for it, if you say the word," put in Timmy.

" I'll do my best," promised Sallie, who had only the vaguest idea of Georgia's intentions.

" I guess I should do better if we had real eats at the first meeting," giggled Montana Marie.

No one paid any attention to her frivolity. Susanna wondered politely why college girls should bother about votes, when of course they couldn't vote yet a while. Georgia explained that working women's rights were just as interesting and important as suffrage, and that anyway the projected organization was to begin right at home, with the problems of college life.

" You see," she explained, " if women are

maybe going to vote and to learn how to run unions and protect their own interests and look out for their children, why, of course we college people ought to be ready to take hold. But how can we, if we've never had any experience in sticking together and thinking about the public good? So what we thought of—only I was just going to explain it all out nicely when most of the crowd had to go up to a mob rehearsal for the senior play—what we thought of was to form a self-government association, to make rules for the college and arrange to carry them out, and—oh, just generally run the ship of state."

"What gorgeousness!" Straight gave a long sigh of admiration. "Why couldn't you think of an elegant scheme like that while we were on hand to profit by it? Freshman year was the time for a thing like that."

"But we hadn't had sociology then," chorused Georgia and Fluffy apologetically.

"Well, don't let's organize it now," pleaded Straight. "It's bad enough to be almost through Harding, and I simply couldn't bear it if I thought that those "—waving comprehensively at the lower class girls—" were still here, going to bed when they were sleepy, and not bothering about cuts or study-hours or any of the other trifling annoyances of Harding life."

"And the next year's freshmen can sit on the note-room table if they want to," giggled Montana Marie joyously.

"Nonsense!" Susanna Hart told her sternly. "That's not a regular rule; it's an unwritten law, and you can't change it any more than you can change the color of your hair."

"Oh!" said Montana Marie slowly. "They write down the rules that everybody knows, and the ones that ——"

"They don't actually write down any of the rules," interrupted Susanna tartly, annoyed at being caught in a contradiction.

"Oh!" repeated Montana Marie. "That's the real difference between college and boarding-school, isn't it? I'm glad I've found out about that at last. But if they're all unwritten rules, and unwritten rules can't be changed, what will be the use of your club? Oh, dear, I promised to be home at five, so I can't wait to have you explain."

"Come to the grand rally to-morrow afternoon," Georgia ordered, "and everything will be revealed. We'll depend on you to get out all the freshmen."

The next day it rained—a fact which, combined with Montana Marie's industry in stirring up the freshmen, and with the prevalent interest in self-government, to produce a mammoth mass-meeting. The Dutton twins, whose method of getting things done, inherited from Madeline Ayres, was to make them seem exclusive and therefore highly desirable, sat in the back row and scoffed at the earnestness with which small points were debated, and at the absurd length of time it took to adopt a simple constitution and elect the smallest possible quota of officers. Georgia Ames was made president. The Duttons resented the reproachful way she stared at them when she introduced Miss Seaton, who spoke on the modern woman so exhaustively that even the admiring Fluffy was finally caught yawning. Next came Betty Wales, who, trying to be brief, left her hearers somewhat confused about the status of self-government, as she had officially investigated it in other colleges for women. And then even the Duttons ceased fidgeting, and, like the other chief organizers, waited breathlessly for Georgia's next announcement, on which, to the initiated, everything depended ; Georgia was to appoint the executive committee, and the executive committee would do the rest ; that is, they would revise the present college rules and have general charge of enforcing the new code. Georgia made a little preliminary speech about President Wallace's faith in the girls and in any experiment that they honestly wanted to try. Then she read the committee list : six prominent girls of the type who could always be relied upon to do the sensible thing, and Fluffy Dutton.

Fluffy jumped up to resign, but Straight persuaded her to wait, and having waited, Fluffy declared that no power on earth should keep her from acting on Georgia's old committee. Before she knew it the committee had elected her chairman.

"That's only so I'll come to all the meetings," grumbled Fluffy. "They're so afraid of not having a quorum."

"I hope you're fixing it about the note-room table," Montana Marie reminded her. "Because if they're all unwritten, I don't see why you can't change one rule as well as another, and I think that one is positively unfair."

"Don't be silly, child," Straight ordered sharply. "Fluffy can't be bothered with any little fiddling custom like the note-room table business. She's fighting the ten o'clock rule. She's been using all her influence to get the committee to report against it, and if she does, and the girls can hereafter use their judgment about going to bed, why, all the bother we've had in organizing and starting the self-government plan going will have been well worth while, in my opinion."

Fluffy sighed. "Maybe," she said. "But I think myself that looking out for your rights is a terrible lot of bother. If you leave it all to the faculty, they manage things fairly well for you, and you have your time free for fun."

"But that's not good sociology, Fluffy," Susanna Hart reminded her with malicious sweetness. "If we're going to learn to help the working women, and to purify politics and so on, we must first understand how to help ourselves and manage our own little republic."

" I suppose so," muttered Fluffy, and went off to a meeting of her hopelessly sensible committee. They had devoted one session each to the various college regulations, had debated them " backward and forward and crisscross," as Fluffy had irritably confided to Straight, and had ended each time by ratifying the existing rule exactly as it stood.

" We don't want to be too radical," the most sensible and the slowest of them all invariably declaimed at each decision. " We don't want to antagonize any one by unnecessary upheavals."

Fluffy had prodded them on, but she had taken no special part in the debates. For if they changed nothing else, she argued, mustn't they in sheer self-defense do away with the ten o'clock rule ? And to-day at last the ten o'clock rule was reached. Naturally Fluffy was worried and irritable. Besides, she had quarreled with Georgia over the make-up of the committee, and she suspected that Georgia had intended the committee to let things alone—that she actually agreed with them about upheavals and being too radical. Fluffy had scorned to ask Georgia a point-blank question about her attitude to the ten o'clock rule.

"Well," said the most hopelessly sensible committee member, when Fluffy had called the session to order, "I suppose the discussion to-day will be more or less of a formality. I don't suppose any of us would consider changing the most important and carefully considered regulation that has been imposed on our college life."

"Is that the—the general sentiment?" asked Fluffy desperately; and was met on all sides by vigorous nods of approval. "Then," she went on hastily, "let's adjourn at once, before it's too late to get a canoe or a tennis court or something else amusing for the rest of the afternoon."

"There's just one thing more," objected the highly sensible member. "I suppose it's understood that, under the self-government plan, we're in honor bound to keep the rules we make. We must provide for a discipline committee to act in cases of carelessness or deliberate disregard, but I'm sure there'll be very little of that sort of thing now that the girls can feel that they're their own lawmakers. Isn't it just splendid that we could put the plan through this year?"

"Is all of that carried?" inquired Fluffy, reckless of parliamentary procedure. "Well, now we can adjourn."

Of the various amusing things with which one may fill a broken afternoon at Harding, Fluffy chose the company of Montana Marie O'Toole and the pursuit of chocolate soda.

"I take back some of what I said about sociology," she told Montana Marie over the soda. "It's interesting and up to date, but it's very misleading. It doesn't tell anything about the bother of protecting your rights. Why, it's even dangerous to try to protect them! Here we are now, honor-bound to keep their old rules—just so much worse off than before. And all because I got excited over the woman question, and Georgia has such a practical mind and loves to try experiments."

But Mary Brooks Hinsdale, having seen the pair through the window and sacrificed her dignity to join them in the pursuit of soda, refused to view the sociological episode as an utter failure.

"Plenty of people would say to you : the moral of that is to let well enough alone," said Mary. "But a much nicer moral, I think, is : try again and you'll come out better. Besides, Fluffy, don't you honestly think that the good old Harding rules work pretty well?"

Fluffy nodded dubiously. "The main thing I've learned," she explained, "is that whatever is worth having in this world—like the right to make your own rules—is a bother to get and a bother to use. But I guess that's no reason for not going in for the worth-while things."

"Let's have another soda all round," suggested Montana Marie.

CHAPTER XVI

THE FRECKLES OF MISS A. PEASE

HARDING COLLEGE had never gone in heavily for track athletics. President Wallace discouraged intercollegiate meets, and class spirit in the matter seemed to be consumed by basket-ball rivalries, with milder interest in the spring term tennis matches. But the affair of the popping mascots rankled in the breasts of the sophomores. They resented the trickery that had lost the Invincibles their game, and they were bent on revenge, slow if need be, but sure and crushing. Only opportunity was lacking. Impulsive spirits had suggested one or two plans, but the class hung back cautiously.

" It must be a sure thing and as hard a hit as they gave us, or it won't do at all," Susanna Hart declared wisely.

In pursuance of this policy the sophomores had waited until May blossoms scented the air

and May langour threatened to dull the edge
of craft and strategy, leaving the freshmen in
complacent possession of their ill-gotten victory. Finally the leading sophomores held a
long and agitated conference under a tree in
Paradise. But nobody had an idea that anybody else considered at all feasible, and they
were about to adjourn in despair when Binks
Ames, who was late as usual, jumped a stone
wall to avoid a détour, and thereby gave Susanna Hart an inspiration.

"There's the track meet. We can beat
them all to pieces at that. We've got splendid runners and jumpers, and they haven't
any who are even passable. We can simply
whitewash them."

"But who cares about a little old track
meet?"

"We can make them care," declared Susanna. "We can talk the subject up and raise
an excitement. We can make track meets
seem as important as basket-ball games. Well,
nearly as important," amended Susanna com-
promisingly.

There was a discouraging lack of response,
but this only irritated Susanna into greater

enthusiasm. "Oh, please don't be so fussy," she begged. "It's our only chance—our very last chance till next year, and paying them up then won't be the same thing at all. It's silly to say that people don't care for track meets. At other colleges they care a lot."

"But it's rather late to begin creating a sentiment for them here," objected a big girl with a provoking drawl in her voice.

"Then we won't begin," retorted Susanna pluckily. "We'll pretend that the sentiment is here already. We'll be amazed—absolutely struck dumb—to find that the freshmen don't understand about it. We will pretty nearly go into hysterics when they say that they haven't yet made up their team. We might suggest combining the meet and the tennis tournament. I've often thought that would be a good idea."

Susanna's determined enthusiasm finally won the day. Anything was better than nothing, and her scheme had no rivals. Accordingly the bewildered freshmen found themselves, an hour or so later, fairly immersed in a strange tide of talk about a track meet. Track meets appeared suddenly to be the end and consummation of the Harding year. Nothing else in spring term mattered. The junior-senior meet was unimportant, like the junior-senior basket-ball game; after you stopped taking "required gym." you naturally lost interest and got out of form. But the freshman-sophomore match was the event of the spring term. Bewildering allusions to broad and high jumps, to dashes, hurdle races, and hammer throws, mingled with ready references to the class champions, Binks and Susanna being prominent among them. It was a flood of sudden, unexpected, overwhelming oratory. The freshmen, dazed and blinded, retired to talk the matter over in private, and the sophomores retired also, to wonder whether they had opened fire too soon, and to arrange a program and assign parts.

"And now for practice. We mustn't take chances. We must do so well that we can't help winning," decreed Susanna inexorably.

Every afternoon, accordingly, the sophomores who could run panted around the track in the hot gymnasium, and those who could jump were busy on the floor with bars and "horses." Every possible candidate was forced to try out her powers. It was to be as complete a "whitewash" of those tricky little freshmen as infinite pains could achieve.

Meanwhile the freshmen consulted with the gym. director, who was secretly amazed and openly delighted at the sudden display of interest in her department. Miss Andrews picked a provisional team, superintended strenuous practice hours, and mingled praise and encouragement with tactful references to the extra year's training and rather exceptional ability of the sophomores—"foemen worthy of your steel, by whom it's an honor to be beaten."

The freshmen managed to see enough of the sophomores' work to understand that their case was indeed hopeless, but they were not at all attracted by the honors of defeat. So they practiced harder than ever and thereby lost their best jumper, who sprained a knee in her frantic efforts to outdo herself.

This was felt by the freshmen to be a crisis. The jumper's room was deluged with violets, and the rest of the team all at once became pampered darlings, for whom no attention was too delicate or too flattering. Even the basket-ball team had never been the center of more anxious consideration.

"It would be a perfect shame to lose." So ran the popular clamor.

"The squad hasn't any hope of winning."

"We beat the Invincibles."

"Let's think up another plan."

"Only it must be an entirely different kind."

"Well, ask Montana Marie. She fixed things up before."

So did public sentiment crystallize, and Montana Marie found herself once more waited upon by a deputation of leading spirits.

"Well, what do you want now?" she demanded gaily. "A way to beat those horrid sophs? But I never have ideas like that. Ask Fluffy Dutton—oh, she's on their side. The other plan wasn't my idea, was it? I just had the general idea of rattling the Invincibles. Couldn't we rattle the squad? Oh, you don't want to repeat yourselves. Then I should think you'd be willing to be beaten. If you win, you repeat."

Montana Marie lapsed into meditative silence, watching the discussion as it wavered to and fro among her guests. But at the first pause she broke into speech again.

" Can't you jump and run and so on ? " she demanded of a sleek, sweet-faced, pink-and-white little girl named Amelia Pease.

Amelia shook her head, smiling gently. " No, of course not. I can't do anything in gym. I guess you weren't in my division."

Montana Marie considered, frowning abstractedly. " No, I wasn't—oh, I know now ! It was a girl named Pease in Miss Mallon's Select School pour les Americaines. She looked like you, too, only she had freckles and you're all peaches and cream."

Amelia blushed at finding herself obliged to own to a connection with Marie's " gay Paree." " That's my twin sister, I suppose. She didn't care for college, so mother sent her abroad instead of keeping her on at prep. school. She's very athletic."

Montana Marie laughed. " Her name is Aurelia, isn't it? I should say she is very athletic. She used to get into awful scrapes sliding down banisters and vaulting tennis nets, and once she got caught turning handsprings in the dormitory, with all our pillows piled on the floor to soften it."

Amelia smiled faintly. " Yes, she's a dreadful tomboy. She is a little stupider at books than I am, but I've always envied her because she was fine at something, instead of just poking along the way I do. She's just back from Paris now, and she's coming up to visit me pretty soon."

" Then you'd better scrub off her freckles and let her jump for the freshmen," suggested Montana Marie with the casual air of a person saying something trivial and rather foolish.

But the leading spirits, who had had not the least doubt that Betty's queer freshman would somehow save the class again, exchanged delighted glances, and then burst into a flood of questions.

" Why couldn't we ? "

" Can't people really tell you apart, Amelia ? "

" But what scrubs off freckles ? I never found anything that——"

" Would it be playing quite fair to use an outsider ? "

" Oh, we'd own up afterward," explained

somebody, "when we'd laughed at them a lot and got them properly sorry for the fuss they're making over track meets."

"If we couldn't get Aurelia's freckles off, we could paint some on Amelia," suggested somebody else.

"Nobody can tell us apart except by the freckles," Amelia assured them.

"Then of course we can do it," cried everybody at once.

Amelia was summarily ordered to send for her twin, who was to arrive exactly two days before the meet, spending the interval in training for the jumps, and, if possible, in getting rid of her freckles. Meanwhile the team was to be taken into the secret, and Rita Carson, who was wonderful about stage make-ups, was to be instructed to try her hand at freckles. Amelia reluctantly consented to be freckled if necessary.

"Only she must use something that comes off easily," she stipulated. "If I can't have the fun that Aurelia does out of tearing around in the sun, why, I don't want my complexion ruined—no, not even to win the track meet."

With Amelia's consent assured, Rita Carson

was the incalculable element in the situation. Rita was artistic, and she had the artistic temperament strongly developed; which meant that she would make freckles wonderfully or not at all, that she could never be relied upon to keep an engagement, and that she was more likely than not to be missing on the crucial day of the track meet. But as it was a case of Rita or nobody, there was nothing to do but try to keep her interested, and hope that possibly the Paris sojourn had bleached out Aurelia.

Aurelia's letter soon settled that : " I'll come and do the jumps for you. All of my beauty spots (and a few more) came back on shipboard. I'd do quite a lot for you, but I draw the line at puttering any more over my face.

" P. S. They're mostly on my forehead— small and millions of them."

A week before the track meet Rita began freckling Amelia according to her twin's general instruction. Various persons exclaimed over the way Amelia's lovely white skin was getting sun-spotted. Amelia replied sweetly that skin like hers generally freckled in summer. To give color to this theory she spent

her afternoons walking, canoeing, or driving
without a hat, which was good Harding custom, but repugnant to poor Amelia. Another
bother was having to put on a hot gym. suit
in the middle of the afternoon and pretend to
practice with the team, to the list of which her
name had been added. Miss Andrews protested vaguely, but as she had suddenly decided to go abroad for the summer, she was too
busy getting ready to take much interest in
the freshman champions.

But the crowning horror of her situation
Amelia found in the restrictions put upon
face-washing.

"One wash a day." Rita Carson was inexorable. "It's absurd of you to insist upon
being made up as often as that, and more I
simply won't do."

This seemed reasonable enough, but Amelia
tearfully declared that she never washed her
face less than four times daily. "And being
in the sun so much gets me hot, and the paint
feels sticky, and I'm just miserable," she wailed
mournfully.

"You're not game for things," Rita told her
crossly. "You agreed to this plan, and you

can't be any sicker of your bargain than I am. When your twin comes you'll only have to go to classes. You can wash your face all the afternoon and evening if you want to, pussy-cat."

"I shall be off the campus then," Amelia retorted with dignity. "It's been thought simpler for us to room together up on Main Street, so you'll have a nice walk before break-fast for a day or two."

Aurelia's arrival was of course kept in the secret, while Amelia's departure from the campus was easily explained on the ground of her wanting to be well rested for the meet. In the morning Amelia, duly freckled, went to classes, while Aurelia, too amused to protest, was locked into their room in hiding. In the afternoon Amelia hid, while Aurelia, escorted and surrounded by a watchful band of the initiated, went to practice. Her performances delighted the escort so extravagantly that they took her for a motor ride, showed her Paradise from a canoe, and promised her wonderful "eats" and "the time of her freckled life" as soon as the meet was over and the secret out. Meanwhile Amelia, who had "kept on" her

freckles in order to make a necessary trip to
the library, waited in vain for a chance to go
out; and with the prospect of a total failure
before her she got up the next morning in an
extremely bad temper. Rita Carson was in a
bad temper too—she was not used to getting
up so early. To tease Amelia, she put the
twins in a row and matched freckle to freckle
with painstaking, maddening slowness. Then
she daubed two huge ones on Amelia's nose,
for good measure, and departed, calling back
a final warning against water.

"But I could wash my nose without doing
any harm, couldn't I, Aurelia?" asked Amelia
indignantly.

Aurelia burst into an annoying peal of
laughter. "I don't know, I'm sure. Better
not take the risk. Oh, Amelia, you look perfectly killing—so exactly like me. Come to
the glass and see."

Amelia refused to be comforted. "I can
see those two freckles all the time," she complained. "They worry me to death. I'd like
to wash the whole thing off and—and ——"

"Think what fun you'll be having to-morrow," suggested Aurelia artfully. "And think

how the class is depending on you. And above everything, don't cry."

Amelia finally departed for the campus, her freckles intact, her nerves unstrung, and a wet wad of handkerchief " to use when she just couldn't stand it any longer " clutched defiantly in her hot little hand.

But if it hadn't been for Montana Marie all might still have been well. Amelia " flunked dead" in her first class, and she looked so wan and woebegone over it that Montana Marie thought it would be only decent to try to cheer her up. She caught up with her between College Hall and the Morton, and drew her out of the crowd to congratulate her on Aurelia's perfectly splendid records. Just then a big bottle-fly came buzzing along, preceding Straight Dutton like a noisy herald. Amelia struck out at it vigorously with her wet handkerchief, and somehow in her excitement hit her own nose instead of the fly. Naturally, off came the two big freckles.

" Oh, stop ! " cried Montana Marie, her eyes wide with horror. " Stop ! You're losing them ! "

" Losing what ? " demanded Straight, joining them. Being Straight, she would probably have guessed at once, but Amelia saved her the trouble by letting fall two big tears and then dabbling wildly at the tears and the freckles, which mingled in a sticky brownish fluid on her peach-blossom cheeks.

Straight stared at the strange spectacle in absolute mystification, and Montana Marie boldly decided that the situation was not yet desperate.

"I told you not to fuss with any of those horrid face-washes," she reproached the choking Amelia. "Freckles aren't the worst thing in the world. You'll be lucky if you haven't ruined your pretty complexion. As for the freckles, I'll bet they're all back by afternoon, don't you, Straight?"

Straight watched them go with vague stirrings of remorse, which dulled her suspicions. Amelia Pease was rather a goose, but it was mean to have gotten the freshmen so worked up and nervous over the meet. Spring term was meant for fun, not for strenuous, nerve-racking contests that brought tears and heart-burnings in their train.

But that afternoon it was a very trim, very

alert, and perfectly self-possessed Miss A. Pease who jumped nonchalantly over the records and turned the sophomore audience pale with rage and dismay. The other freshman athletes did well too; even without Miss A. Pease the meet was no sophomore walk-over, and with her it was an overwhelming freshman victory.

" Just the same," complained Susanna Hart irritably, " they needn't act as if it was all so comical. They needn't have hysterics once in about five minutes. They needn't shriek with mirth every time they look at me."

As a matter of fact, the joke connected with the freckles of Miss A. Pease was being passed along the freshman ranks, preparatory to its being spread still further. The freshmen had decided that, with Straight Dutton knowing more than she ought, the safest as well as the most dramatic procedure would be to let the cat out of the bag the minute the final score had been announced. Accordingly the freshman president rose promptly, called for silence, and with much dignity made her startling statement.

" Owing to a possibly regrettable mistake

we are obliged to withdraw the scores of Miss
A. Pease. That leaves the victory with the
sophomore team. We congratulate them
heartily, and "—with a sudden change of
tone—" here comes the mistake. Wouldn't
you have made it too, if you could?"

This was a signal for Montana Marie to lead
the Pease twins into the center of the field—
Amelia again carefully freckled and dressed
exactly like her sister.

"Alike as two Pease in a pod," cried some
would-be wit.

"Bully joke!" acknowledged a group of
generous sophomores.

"Too good to keep to ourselves," shrilled
back Montana Marie.

"Who makes freckles? Rita Carson, she
makes freckles," chanted a riotous freshman
chorus.

"Freckles that will come off," added the
enlightened Straight.

In a minute the field was pandemonium,
with the Peases and Rita Carson being carried
round it on freshman shoulders, and the
sophomores clamoring eagerly for the whole
story.

"It's not so bad," admitted Susanna magnanimously. "We've got you on muscle, but I'm afraid you've got us on brains. So honors are easy, and—oh, we've got another year coming!" concluded Susanna with a joyous little sigh.

CHAPTER XVII

At last Bob Parker had got what she wanted. Babe brought her up to Harding for what they called "one last frisk," in a big motor-car, with a shiny hat trunk strapped impressively on behind, and the most wonderful tea-basket to take off on the numerous picnics which were to be the "frisk's" chief feature, because Bob doted on them so.

"It's a newsboys' club to run just as I like," Bob explained around the festive board of picnic number one. "It has a splendid building in town, and a farm for summers that I made father give me. How's that for little me?"

"But I don't see how she's ever going to get away for any more fun," Babe told them anxiously.

"I shall have my fun as I go along, silly," Bob retorted promptly. "When you find a job that really fits, you don't need to worry about vacations, do you, Betty Wales?"

"Why don't you ask me?" demanded Madeline gaily. "I'm the one who's really perfectly crazy about her work."

"I notice you take plenty of vacation," Babe told her.

"That," said Madeline, "is because I'm naturally idle and frivolous. Bob, being naturally serious-minded and industrious, will do differently, without sacrificing her happiness."

"Calling one of the three little B's industrious and serious-minded!" mocked Babbie. "How absurd! But it isn't any absurder, maybe, than the way the three little B's have settled down since they left college. Just think! By next fall two of them will be staid married ladies ——"

"And the third will be wedded to a great career," Madeline took her up. "Of course I'm always more interested in the great careers. It's dreadful to belong to such a marrying bunch as this is. Any day I expect to find myself alone in the state of single blessedness."

"You're not worrying about that very much yet a while, are you?" Rachel demanded laughingly.

"Not really losing sleep over it," Madeline acknowledged. "So far I feel that I can safely count on you and Christy and Roberta, and Bob—though for all I know there may be a man behind her fondness for newsboys' homes. I have my suspicions that there's a man behind Helen Adams' sudden enthusiasm for teaching, and I have my grave doubts about Betty Wales. So far the two parties are about even, but the O. M.'s are bound to lose out in the end, poor dears!"

"Well, anyway, we have enough weddings to arrange for this summer," sighed Babbie Hildreth. "I certainly think we ought to make out our schedule of dates right away now, while we're here together."

"Do stop talking about that wedding schedule, Babbie," protested Babe. "It sounds exactly like a matrimonial bureau."

"Well, what's the matter with matrimonial bureaus?" Madeline came gaily to Babbie's rescue. "Aren't we all disciples of Betty's congenial occupation theory? And isn't marriage a congenial occupation for more of us than any other one pursuit? I think that Betty ought to establish a matrimonial bureau-department in her famous Congenial Employment Agency."

" I will," laughed Betty, " if you'll run it."

"Oh, let me run it," begged Babe. " I should love to make matches. Only I'm not a bit businesslike. Father Morton says —— Good gracious! That reminds me of something." Babe's face was a study in dismay. " Father Morton had dinner with us the day I wired Bob about coming up for this ' frisk.' When he heard about it he said he'd come too, but then he remembered he couldn't, so he sat down at my desk and wrote a letter to Betty. Goodness, how he did rage about my stub pens! He traced all the troubles of modern civilization to stub pens."

" And did he stop writing the letter because the pens didn't suit?" inquired Betty mildly.

Babe started. " I told you I wasn't businesslike. I go off so on tangents. Yes, he finished the letter with John's fountain pen — which he also raged at—and gave it to me to take to you. He said it was important. It's in my shopping bag this minute, just where I put it when he gave it to me. We'd better go right back and find it—we ought to, anyway, because it's getting dark, and my man doesn't know the road. Wouldn't Father Morton be up in the air if he knew I'd forgotten his important letter all this long time?"

A search of Babe's shopping bag disclosed no letter, important or otherwise. A general shake-up of her luggage also failed to bring to light the missing communication. Finally, under protest, Babe opened the shiny hat trunk, and there right on top was the letter, fat and imposing in its long, official-looking envelope.

"Oh, I remember now," Babe confessed. "I put it in there on purpose, so I'd be sure to see it when I took out my best hat. As if anybody ever wore best hats, or any hats, in this lovely, comfortable spot! I'm very sorry, Betty, though I always think it does Father Morton good to be kept waiting."

Betty laughed. "Then I shall put all the blame on you," she said, and took her letter and Madeline off to the Tally-ho, where a big dinner with features for the following night made necessary a conference between the manager and her chief furnisher of inspirations.

"May I just glance at this letter before

we talk?" asked Betty. " You'll excuse me, won't you, Mad? He probably wants me to kidnap you and make you invent another ploshkin, whether you want to or not."

As Betty read, her expression grew serious, then amazed, then almost frightened. " What do you think now, Mad? He wants us to come and start another barn tea-shop for him round the corner from Fifth Avenue—oh, Madeline, in almost the very place we wanted when we started the Tally-ho—only of course we never thought then of looking around for a barn. And Madeline, what put it into his head was a letter he had from a department store in Chicago, wanting us to plan a tea-room for them,—with features. Mr. Morton thinks we'd better keep our ideas for our own use."

" Certainly," agreed Madeline, as calmly as if opening a tea-shop off Fifth Avenue was an every-day occurrence. "Tea-rooms aren't like ploshkins. If you make them too popular, you spoil them. We can call the new place the Coach and Four."

"Then you think we can really start it?" asked Betty anxiously.

" Easily," returned Madeline. " We can manage the two places beautifully. You'll have to go down right away and get things going. We can have our old Washington Square cook, I'm almost sure. When I'm in New York I'll manage to be there a lot, and —we shan't open till fall, I should say, so why not get Fluffy Dutton, who is planning to waste her talents teaching the Young Idea, to come and do the Proper Excitement act for the Coach and Four ? "

" And Georgia, who is also going to teach, to do the hard, steady grind," added Betty.

Madeline looked at her quizzically. " The hard, steady grind that you've always had to do for the Tally-ho," she said repentantly. " I'm sorry I'm such a flyaway, Betty."

Betty laughed at Madeline's woebegone expression. " I'm not," she said. " You're a genius, and I rather think Fluffy is one too. I don't mind the hard, steady pulling. I rather like it—generally. But I can't be doing it in two places at once."

Madeline nodded. " I know. There's a lot of hard, steady grind to every book I write— along with a pinch or two, maybe, of the queer thing called genius. The grind in the books I do myself, because I have to, and it's fun—the long, steady pull up to that lovely stopping place called Finis. I say, Betty, this old-maid business isn't so bad. Just think of all the fun we've had doing things, and all the fun we're going to have with the Coach and Four. Those others give up a lot for a mere man."

Betty smiled indulgently at Madeline's declaration of independence. "If it hadn't been for a mere man named Morton, the Tally-ho would have gone to smash long ago," she reminded her. "Mary Brooks hasn't stopped doing interesting things because she's married, and Babe could do anything she liked—have half a dozen tea-shops, if she wanted them. Mr. Morton would give them to her like that! Only of course you've got to find the right man."

Madeline said nothing to that; she only watched Betty's face suddenly take on its sober, far-away, grown-up look, and wondered what that meant.

Presently Betty came out of her brown study.

"'Coach and Four might do for name. Down Thursday with Miss Ayres to talk things over and begin arrangements.' Does that sound like a businesslike telegram, Madeline? And will you surely go on Thursday? You must promise fair and square, because Mr. Morton perfectly hates to be disappointed. Well then, come with me to the telegraph office."

"I wouldn't give much for Jim Watson's chances," Madeline told Babe, who was sharing her room, later the same evening. "She is too happy as she is. I tell you, Babe, when a girl has found her niche, and it's as big as Betty's is and is going to be, it takes an extra-specially wonderful man to carry her off her feet."

Babe sniffed. "It's quite evident you've never been in love, Madeline Ayres."

"I've written some stunning love-scenes," Madeline retorted with a grin.

"If you think that's the same thing, you can just wait," Babe told her loftily.

"All right," said Madeline. "I shall have to, I guess. Incidentally I know something that will make you stare and be glad you

know such distinguished and brilliant old
maids as Betty and me."

" What? " demanded Babe, vastly excited.

" Can't tell you yet a while."

" Why not ? "

" Because Betty said not to."

Babe shrugged her shoulders with a fine
assumption of indifference.   " It can't be that
she's engaged, after what you've said ; so I
don't care much about knowing."

" Wait till you see It."

Babe was too proud to ask any more questions, but she lay awake for hours trying to
guess what It could be.   Meanwhile Betty
Wales was dreaming wild dreams, at the
climax of which the dashing Coach and Four
ran over Jim Watson.

CHAPTER XVIII

Mr. Morton answered Betty's telegram with another :

"Coach and Six not a bit too big for my notions. Thursday O. K. for me. Young Watson to plan improvements. Depend on you to keep him docile."

Madeline, being inspired by the evident largeness of Mr. Morton's notions, retired at once to the Tally-ho loft to meditate on delightful possibilities, and to sketch posters and a hanging sign for the Coach and Six. But presently her eye happened to fall upon Thomas, the door-boy, and in a moment the posters for the Coach and Six were forgotten, and Madeline was off in hot pursuit of green broadcloth.

"Take off your coat so I can use it for a pattern," she ordered the bewildered Thomas on her return. "No, I suppose you can't do without a coat very well. Sprint home and get another suit that fits you. Tell your mother I won't hurt it. Hurry now."

"The idea!" she told Betty while she waited for Thomas. "We've had that boy here for six months and never once thought to dress him up in Lincoln green, like a postboy. Never mind! We need some new features for commencement. We can't have 19— think we're just resting on our laurels. I'll make new tea menus to match Thomas— little riding-crops painted across the top, with real green ribbon rosettes stuck on the handles. Or why not have real little riding-crops? Thomas can whittle them out in his idle moments."

In vain Betty suggested that the Tally-ho was well enough as it was, and that the plans for the Coach and Six must be well advanced by Thursday or Mr. Morton would be impatient and annoyed. Madeline calmly branched out on to fairy menus for the Peter Pan annex, and then became completely absorbed in a fairy play suggested to her by the menus. She was persuaded to keep the Thursday appointment in New York only because she wanted to read the play to Agatha

Dwight. Betty, who had been busy all the week with plans and estimates, memoranda of " things we ought to have," " things to speak to Jim about," " necessary glass and silver," and so on, was duly grateful that Madeline consented to accompany her on any pretext; for when Madeline was once on the ground, with the actual site of the Coach and Six, Jim's ideas, and Mr. Morton's fury of energy to inspire her, Betty knew she would forget even the fairy play and plan a tea-shop that would dazzle " little old New York."

And she did. Jasper J. Morton followed her delightedly about all day, his eyes twinkling and his dry laugh cackling out at her queer, unsystematic methods of work. He went with her to choose furniture, to interview the famous Mr. Enderby, who, quite overcome by the awe-inspiring combination of the irresistible Madeline Ayres and the great Mr. Morton, promised to design anything from walls to menus; and finally they rode off together to engage the Washington Square cook, who blandly ignored the great Mr. Morton, but promised to come and cook in his tea-shop any time " if you axes me, Miss

Madeline, an' bring a black kitten as usual, if so desired."

By the time he had watched Madeline order livery for the porters, design costumes for the maids, pick out china, and overturn all Jim's plans because the fireplace wasn't quite big enough to please her, Mr. Morton turned to Betty with a sigh of admiration.

"She's a steam-engine, that girl. She could tire me out, I guess. See here, I guess she keeps you fairly busy, picking up after her, like. She's the beginning kind—don't wait to put on any finishing touches. All right. We'll hire two or three finishers to go round after her. She'd make several fortunes for anybody that could manage her right. See here, Miss Ayres, couldn't you wind up the day by inventing another of those splasher novelties?"

Madeline shook her head laughingly. "I'm going to dinner now with Agatha Dwight. I want to read her a play I've just written."

So Mr. Morton bore off Betty and Jim for dinner with him. During the dessert he discovered an opportune acquaintance at the next table, who kept him talking so long that

Betty had to interrupt them to say good-bye, and Jim had to take Betty to her train. She had wanted to stay over a day for spring shopping, but there was a Student's Aid trustee-meeting the next morning, and the secretary must be on hand to report.

It was nearly half-past ten when Betty drove up to the campus. She dismissed her carriage at the little gate close to Morton Hall, which, to her amazement, was still ablaze with lights. In a minute she remembered why; it was the evening of the Belden-Morton play. Betty hurried up the walk, anxious to hear how it had gone off. She thought the door might still be open, and she tried it before she went down to the end of the piazza to tap, as she had arranged to do, on Mrs. Post's sitting-room window. There was a light in the room, but the shade was up, and between the hanging curtains Betty could see that the room was empty, and the bedroom beyond dark. Evidently Mrs. Post was talking over the play with her girls, utterly forgetful of her promise to let Betty in. So Betty went back to the door and rang, and, as it was rather a shivery spring night, she tramped down the piazza again while she waited for somebody to come and open the door. As she turned the corner she heard voices, and saw a man leading two saddle-horses and a girl in a black dress and white cap and apron—evidently one of the Morton Hall maids—come up a path that led through the shrubberies between Morton Hall and the Students' Building, where the play had been given.

"I think we should try it over," the man was saying as they stopped in a patch of light by the back door.

"No indeed! How absurd you are, dear," tittered the girl. "The idea of rehearsing a thing like —— "

"Oh, Miss Wales! Come right in out of the cold, you poor child." Mrs. Post's kindly voice broke into the tête-à-tête by the back door. "I'm so sorry I forgot you. Come and have some supper and hear about the wonderful play. I'm giving the girls a little treat to make them sleep better after all the excitement."

The Belden-Morton production of "The Purple Ribbon" had been a grand success. Georgia Ames, Fluffy Dutton, and the Mystery had collaborated in writing it, and the

program announced that it was a subtle combination of Shaw, Shakespeare, and Sherlock
Holmes. The Morton Hall half of the cast,
still in make-up and costumes, lined up for
Betty's appreciative inspection. The Thorn
was the villain of the piece, in very elegant
evening clothes and curling black moustaches.
The twin Digs figured respectively as the villain's innocent young accomplice (white flan-
nels and very pink cheeks), and the heroine's
mother-in-law (Mrs. Post's second best black
silk, a bonnet with strings, and white mitts).
The Mystery had fairly insisted that the
freckle-faced girl who roomed next to her
should have a part, "because she wants it so
awfully much." So she had been cast for the
Enigma, who had nothing particular to do
but wear a blank and unintelligent expression and say, "Is it so?" at intervals. This
she had done so effectively that she had made
the hit of the evening. Mrs. Post and the
none-acting members of Morton Hall explained all this eagerly to Betty, and then
Connie was called into the line because she
had been the Bell and the Noise Without.

"And I was the only one of the cast that

had to be prompted," Connie confessed sadly. " I was thinking how awfully pretty my room-mate looked in black, and if Georgia hadn't poked me hard —— "

" Why, where's Amanda O'Toole?" cut in the Thorn suddenly. " She was Amanda the maid, Miss Wales, and she did look too cute —— Oh, there you are, Marie. Come and let Miss Wales see how you look in the raiment of servitude."

Marie had borrowed her costume complete from the obliging Belden House Annie, adding nothing but a dashing moline bow under her chin.

" Ain't she the prettiest Amanda that ever came down the pike?" quoted the Thorn from her part, with a genial twirl of her huge moustaches.

" I sure am, but it's no concern of yours, Monsieur," retorted Marie, from her part, flirting her black skirt coquettishly as she made for a plate of sandwiches. " Isn't Mrs. Post the nice lady? I'm as hungry as a bear— I couldn't eat any dinner because I was so excited about the play."

" If you were so hungry, why didn't you

come in here sooner?" demanded the Thorn incisively. "The rest of us are all through eating."

"Oh, I was fussing around. This is the first time I was ever on the stage, you see, and I'm that rattled." Montana Marie took a huge bite out of one of Mrs. Post's ginger-cookies by way of closing the discussion.

Betty went to bed humming a gay little tune. She was thinking of the house-play that Roberta Lewis had starred in so splendidly years ago, of the Coach and Six, of the Student's Aid meeting in the morning,—she must get up early to write her report,—and finally of Jim Watson's comical struggle between strong personal annoyance at her having added another to her too-numerous interests and responsibilities and his equally strong artistic approval of Madeline's ideas for the Coach and Six and of Mr. Morton's lavishness in carrying them out.

"I smell lilacs!" Betty decided suddenly, and turning off her lights she leaned far out into the dark, eagerly drinking in the sweet spring odors. And then, as her eyes fell on the patch of light by the back door, she re-

membered the anxious groom and the tittering
maid, whom she had heard arguing by the
back porch, and she wondered idly what kind
of thing it was you didn't rehearse, in the
opinion of said tittering maid. Probably she
had been telling the groom all about the play,
and they were discussing some point in the
plot. The maids were always as keen as the
girls about the house-plays. Then she wondered, thinking of the two saddle-horses, if the
Moonshiners' riding club had been revived,
and she decided to ask Georgia if she might
go off on some of their spring trips. Harding
was so lovely in the spring—no other place
was quite like it. But—those Student's Aid
trustees met at ten o'clock sharp. Betty reso-
lutely dismissed plays and picnics and the
disturbing scent of lilacs from her mind, and
courted sleep; for her alarm clock was set for
six and she must be ready for a hard morning's
work.

It was an exciting day, altogether. One of
the Student's Aid trustees had secured a big
gift for the Association. In return she wanted
to dictate important policies, and particularly
to lay out the secretary's work. The other

trustees resented her assumption of superior authority. Both factions took Betty into their confidence. One insisted on giving her lunch; the other asked her to dinner. Mr. Morton telegraphed for impossible details. Mrs. Post had hit upon this busiest day of the year for cleaning Betty's room. Feeling very young and inadequate, and very, very sleepy, Betty escaped as soon as possible from the trustees' dinner, put a " Do not disturb " sign on her door and went to bed.

The pale morning sun was creeping faintly in at her window, though she was sure she hadn't been asleep ten minutes, when somebody knocked on her door. Somebody had to keep on knocking for an embarrassing interval before Betty woke up enough to realize what was happening, and to open the door. Connie stood outside. She was attired in a scarlet silk kimono, the gift of her generous but thoughtless roommate. For Connie's washed-out hair had a decided suspicion of red in its dull tints, and her complexion was the sort that went with red hair and should never go with a scarlet kimono. In the dim light of the corridor her sallow, anxious little face looked frightened and quite ghostly.

"Did I wake you up, Miss Wales?" she demanded stupidly. "It's four o'clock in the morning. I saw your 'Don't disturb' sign, but I suppose it was meant for last night. Besides I—you see, Miss Wales, Marie has disappeared."

Betty stifled a tremendous yawn and tried to consider Connie's news with becoming seriousness.

"I'm afraid I don't understand," she said at last. "You mean she isn't in your room? Are you sure she isn't in some one's else?"

Connie nodded. "Yes—she—I'm quite sure, Miss Wales. She's disappeared."

"When?" asked Betty, who was wide awake now.

"I don't know, Miss Wales. About ten was when I really saw her last. She had a chafing-dish party last night. I was studying with Matilda Jones. I kept expecting Marie to come for me, as she usually does just before they disperse, to have some of the refreshments. When the ten-minute bell rang, I went to our room. She was there, but she went right out for something. When she came back it was after ten, so she undressed in the dark. At least I supposed she undressed. When I woke up just now she was gone."

"Oh, well," said Betty pleasantly, "she's somewhere in the house, of course. She ought to be in her room in bed, but ——"

"Her saddle and that big felt hat she wears when she rides, and her corduroy suit have disappeared too, Miss Wales."

Betty started. "They have? Then she's probably gone on some early-morning riding-party. Oh, dear, those crazy girls! What won't they think of next?"

"I don't believe it's a regular riding-party, Miss Wales. From things Marie has been saying lately, I think it's an elopement."

Betty's eyes grew round, and her voice quivered with anxiety. "Please tell me all that you know about it, Miss Payson, as quickly as you can. There may be no time to lose." Betty closed the door softly and began hurriedly to put on her clothes, while she listened to Connie's story.

"Well," began Connie eagerly, "she's been

writing letters lately—oh, quantities of them ! She always writes a good many, but lately she's spent most of her time at it. And she's cut classes a good deal. She's never done that before. And a few days ago she gave me six of her dresses—two perfectly new ones. She said she shouldn't want so many clothes much longer. Then day before yesterday a man came to call. I heard the girls say it was the same one she was with the night of the prom. She was very much excited that evening, and it wasn't about the play, because when I spoke about that to her she didn't know what I meant at first, and then she said, 'Oh, the play !' as if it wasn't of any consequence to her. Yesterday morning when I came into our room after a class she was rolling a lot of things up in her raincoat. I asked her what in the world she was doing, and she—she kissed me "—Connie blushed at the intimate confession—" and said she was just seeing how much you could tie on to a saddle, because some one had asked her to find out. And now "—Connie's lips and voice quivered—" and now she's gone. That's all I know, Miss Wales. I think she's eloped on horseback with that man from her home in Montana."

"But that would be so perfectly absurd!" Betty was dressed by this time. She twisted her hair into a hasty knot, and put on a droopy hat to hide the snarls. "Have you ever heard Marie speak of riding to any of the little towns around here, Miss Payson? Was she especially fond of any little village near here?"

Connie considered for a minute. "She likes the ride to Gay's Mills, because it's all the way through the woods. And she's been over there twice lately. She went riding day before yesterday,—we all thought it was queer for her to go riding on the day of the play— and I think from something she said that she lost the girl she started out with, and maybe met some one else."

"What girl did she start with?"

Connie mentioned the name of the sophomore who, being proverbially unlucky with horses, had fallen off on the famous Mountain Day ride.

"I see," said Betty curtly. She was perfectly sure that, unless Montana Marie had

meant to lose her, she would never have gone
riding with that particular girl. " Please
telephone Grant's garage," Betty ordered
swiftly. " Tell them to send up a car at once,
and a man who knows the country roads.
Say it's for me. If they object to the early
start tell them it's a matter of vital importance. If that's not enough, hold the wire
and call me. I shall be in Mrs. Post's room.
I hate to bother her, but I can't very well go
alone."

"Couldn't you take me?" asked Connie
eagerly.

Betty considered. " Why—yes—yes, that
might be quite as well. Then you go and get
ready, while I do the telephoning."

Twenty minutes later Connie and Betty
were flying along the road to Gay's Mills. It
was a slender chance, but in the absence of
other clues it must serve. Connie confided to
Betty that she had never been in an automo-
bile before.

" It doesn't matter," Betty told her absently. " Oh, I beg your pardon. I don't
believe I quite understood what you said."

Connie lapsed into rather frightened silence,

and Betty was left free to consider the situation. "Undertaking" Montana Marie O'Toole looked, this morning, like a pretty serious business. If she really had eloped, what would Mrs. O'Toole say? And what would President Wallace think? Not much use getting her through mid-years for an ending like this. But somehow Betty couldn't believe that her freshman would be so foolish. She almost ordered the chauffeur to drive back to the campus; she was sure they would find that Georgia was missing too, and the other riding people. Then suddenly she remembered the maid and the groom, as she had thought them, talking by the Morton House door, and Montana Marie's belated arrival at Mrs. Post's treat. Was an elopement perhaps the kind of thing that you didn't rehearse? Betty's heart sank. Perhaps she ought to have called Mrs. Post and divided responsibilities. Perhaps she ought even to have aroused Prexy. Certainly she ought to have had a better reason than Connie's vague surmises for choosing the Gay's Mills road. The Gay's Mills road turned sharply just then, and Betty saw two horseback riders trotting decorously to meet her--Montana Marie in her Western riding things, including the forbidden magenta handkerchief, and a man whom Connie identified briefly with an excited ungrammatical little squeak.

"It's him!"

CHAPTER XIX

"Sh!" Betty warned her hastily, because of the chauffeur, and leaning forward she ordered him to stop. "I want to speak to those people," she explained briefly.

Just then Montana Marie, who had the sun in her eyes, recognized Betty, and triumphantly announced the discovery to her companion in her shrillest tones. "It's Miss Wales come after us. What did I tell you?"

Then she slipped off her horse, and with the reins thrown over her arm came to meet Betty, while the man from Montana, looking very glum and very foolish, prepared to stay where he was.

But, "Come on, Fred, and meet Miss Wales," Montana Marie commanded imperiously, and he dismounted in turn and followed Marie.

"You needn't have come after us," Marie

311

began smilingly. "We were just going back of ourselves. I happened to think that you wouldn't like it."

"Then you haven't——" began Betty eagerly.

"Haven't eloped?" finished Marie easily. "Oh, no, not yet. We weren't half-way to Gay's Mills when I happened to think how you'd feel. And ever since we've been standing in the road, up there at the top of the hill, arguing about it, haven't we, Fred?"

The boy—he looked younger than Marie—nodded sullenly. "Not arguing exactly," he amended. "You just kept saying over and over that you wouldn't go on."

"Until I'd seen Miss Wales," amended Marie calmly. Then she looked at the car, and, apparently noticing Connie for the first time, called out cheerfully, "Hello, roomie! Too bad I waked you out of your early morning nap with that squeaky door."

"Good-morning," Connie quavered back in a frightened voice.

"We ought to get rid of her and of that chauffeur," declared Marie competently. "Why not all go home now, and then I can come to see you this morning, Miss Wales, whenever you say."

This was such an amazing proposition from the chief eloper, that Betty stared at it for a moment.

"You can trust us to follow right along, Miss Wales," said the man from Montana quietly. "Or better still, Marie can go back with you, and I'll lead her horse home. I guess that's the best way, Marie."

Betty took a sudden liking to the man from Montana. There was something very straightforward and businesslike about him, and his sulks were only natural under the circumstances.

"All right," agreed Marie, having considered the proposal for a moment. "Only give me my saddle-pack. It might jog loose without your noticing, and it has my silver toilette things in it, and all my pictures of you, Fred."

So Montana Marie O'Toole, bearing the precious possessions which, for reasons known only to herself, she had chosen to bring with her on her elopement, placidly took her seat in the tonneau, between Connie and Betty; and all the way home she chatted composedly, instructing Connie in the lore of automobiling—quite as if an early morning elopement (that did not come off) was a part of her daily routine.

"Don't you tell anybody about Fred and me," she ordered Connie, when they were back at the Morton. "And say, take my raincoat and empty it out, before the girls get a chance to see it and wonder what it means. I'm going to talk to Miss Wales."

But once alone with Betty, she broke down and cried, dabbling at the tears with her magenta handkerchief.

"Maybe you think I don't want to marry Fred," she wailed. "Maybe you think I didn't get Ma interested in American colleges on purpose so Fred and I could be nearer together. It takes two weeks for letters from the Bar 4 ranch to get to Paris. Think of the things that can happen on a ranch in two weeks. From Bar 4 to Harding is only four days. Of course a college in Montana would have been still better, but Ma would have seen through that. Oh, dear, what shall I do, Miss Wales?"

"Send your friend about his business, go home in June, tell your mother about your engagement,—if you are engaged,—and have a pretty wedding in your own home, when you and your family decide that it is best for you to be married." Betty was trying hard to act the part of sensible, middle-aged adviser to heedless youth, though she felt extremely unequal to the rôle.

" That sounds lovely," wailed Montana Marie, " but the trouble is, you don't know Ma."

" I know she's very fond of you," began Betty.

" But she's a lot fonder of a ridiculous idea she's got into her head of having me marry a duke, or a prince, or some other horrid little foreigner. That's what she's designed me for, ever since I was born and Pa struck it rich on the same day. She's always thought it was a sort of providence. And my being in love with Fred doesn't make the least particle ef difference to her." Marie sobbed again forlornly. " I 'most wish we had gone right on and got married this morning."

" Oh, no, you don't," Betty assured her earnestly. " Think how ashamed I should have felt, and how all the college would have been talked about and laughed at on your account."

Marie brightened visibly. "I thought of that myself. That's exactly why I wouldn't go on. Out in Montana lots of girls just ride off and get married on the spur of the minute. But it's different here, isn't it? I felt that it was, after we'd started. And it's different with me. After you've been to school in Paris, and to college for nearly a year, and have traveled a lot, you can't do the way you could if you've lived your whole life in a mining camp. I thought when I put on my Western togs that I'd get into the spirit of the occasion, but I didn't. I felt silly."

"Was it your idea?" asked Betty curiously.

"Oh, yes," acknowledged Montana Marie, "it was every bit my idea. Don't you blame it on Fred. His only reason for coming East was to make sure that nobody had cut him out. You see he didn't understand about the businesslike nature of the Prom. Man Supply Company. Miss Wales——"

"Yes."

"Do you suppose you could possibly persuade Ma to let us be married?"

" If you'll send Fred home and finish your year's work here properly, I'll try."

Montana Marie considered. " All right. I can promise that much without any trouble. I told Fred that I'd rather elope out West than here, if we had to do it at all. Ma wants to take me to Europe again for the summer, but I shall just put my foot down that I've got to see my father first. Then if you haven't persuaded her by that time —— Oh, Miss Wales ——"

" Yes," encouraged Betty smilingly.

" If Georgia Ames sent Ma an invitation to commencement, I think she'd come. That would give you a chance to talk to her, and talking is better than writing any day."

Betty agreed that it was.

" And you must talk to Fred before he goes, so you can see what a nice boy he is. Ma ought to see that what we need in our family isn't a silly title nor more money, but brains and good sense and nice manners. Fred has all those."

Betty promised to talk to Fred later in the morning, and Marie prepared to depart. After she had opened the door she came back to ask a final question.

"Miss Wales, when you promised to undertake me last summer, you didn't guess why I wanted to come to Harding College so badly, now did you?"

"Why, no," said Betty. "I thought you were coming for what you could get out of it, —the fun and the experience and the education."

"Whereas," Marie took her up, "I was coming to be nearer to Fred, and to have a chance to marry him. But I did get the fun and the experience and the education too. So you haven't wasted your time, Miss Wales." Montana Marie held up her flower-like face for a kiss.

Up in her own room Montana Marie changed into a linen dress, discoursing meanwhile to Connie on the merits of a college education. "Concentration is all right. That is going to come in handy whatever we do later. But the best thing about a college education is the way you have to live up to it. So many people are nice to you and help you along. You can't make them sorry they did it. All my life people are going to find out that I was at Harding for a year—

well, at least a year," put in Marie hastily.
"And after the royal way I've been treated
here, I've got to live up to Harding. I wish
I'd thought of that sooner, but I was certainly
lucky to think of it when I did."

Later she expatiated upon the same thesis
to Betty and the man from Montana, whom
she had conducted to Betty's office for the
promised interview.

"Maybe," said the boy with a whimsical
smile, "maybe I'm not up to Harding standards, Marie. This year at college has
changed you—I can see that. Maybe I'm
not ——"

"Nonsense!" cut in Marie, and slammed
the door after herself. The next minute she
stuck her head in to say, "If you're not up
to them, you'll have to improve, that's all.
Because you and I ——" she backed out and
shut the door—softly this time.

That night Straight Dutton trilled outside
Betty's window. "Come out for a speck of a
stroll," she begged. "It's lovely lilac-scented
moonlight out here, and I've got a jist to tell
you. It's about your freshman."

Wondering anxiously if Montana Marie's

attempt at an elopement could have been discovered, Betty hurried out to meet Straight.

"I've discovered why she came to Harding," Straight began with gratifying promptness. "And it's just as queer and ridiculous as you'd expect her reason for doing a good sensible thing to be."

"Yes?" queried Betty, her heart sinking lower with Straight's every word. If Straight knew, all the college knew. Even if the newspapers didn't get hold of it, it was bad enough; and if they did ――――

"How did you find out, Straight?" she asked desperately.

"She told me." Straight was too much amused by the absurdity of the reason to notice Betty's perturbation. "She didn't mean to tell, but I got it out of her."

Betty met this disclosure in annoyed silence.

"Want to guess?" asked Straight gaily. "But you never could. She came to learn American slang, so she can fascinate the French nobility with it. She says they all adore American slang. She says I have taught her more than any other one person, and so when she's married to a count or a

duke or an earl—what's a French earl, Betty?
—she's going to ask me to the wedding to
show her undying gratitude. Isn't that
absurd? And yet she means every word of
it."

"Oh, Straight, dear!" Betty laughed at
her merrily. "What perfect nonsense! Even
Montana Marie isn't so absurd as that. She
was paying you up for the weird tales of
Harding customs that you told her last fall."

"Oh, I don't think so," said Straight positively. "She's forgotten all about those
weird tales. Well, if this isn't her real reason,
I'll bet the real one is just as comical. Montana Marie O'Toole never struggled into Harding College just to learn a little Latin and less
Greek."

"Maybe not," agreed Betty solemnly.
"Very likely you're right, Straight."

"When I flap my invitation to the duke's
wedding in your face," declared Straight
solemnly, "then you'll see that I am. Fluff
and Georgia and Timmy and I are compiling
her a dictionary of slang for our parting
present."

"Be sure you dedicate it ' To the Champion

Bluffer,'" advised Betty, her eyes dancing at
the thought of Straight's probably speedy
disillusion. "And now I must really go in,
Straight. I have dozens of things to do."

"Wait a minute," Straight begged, desperate
in her turn. "Betty Wales, twins are twins.
If Georgia and Fluff are going to be in a
wonderful new tea-shop in New York, what's
to become of me? Can't there be a place for
me too? Fluffy won't do anything unless I'm
there to keep her cheerful and help her decide
things. Can't there be a place for me too? I
know I'm not clever like Fluffy, nor pretty.
My—hair—doesn't—curl. But twins are
twins, Betty Wales."

Betty patted her shoulder comfortingly.
"I'll think. If Emily Davis goes back to
teaching, perhaps Georgia could be here, and
you and Fluff—or you two could be here.
Well, I'll think, Straight. I ought to have
thought sooner. I wish I had a twin to keep
me cheerful and help me decide things. I
need one this minute worse than Fluffy ever
did in her life. Now I must go."

Straight stared after her wonderingly.
"She needs a twin! Good gracious! If she

was twins, I guess there isn't anything in the world she couldn't do. And yet for all she's such a winner, she knows what it means to be just a plain straight-haired twin like me. She'll manage about fixing a place for me. And she shan't ever be sorry she did. Now I can go to the last meeting of the Why-Get-Up-to-Breakfast Club and be the life of the party."

Meanwhile Betty Wales, quite appalled by the day's complications, was getting them off her mind by writing to Jim. " Here are a few of the things I have on hand just now," she wrote. " Stopping elopements, deciding on the eligibility of strange suitors, persuading eccentric mothers to let their daughters marry, fitting two twins into the position that one twin will fill. So of course I can't come to New York again until after commencement, and you must persuade Mr. Morton that it doesn't matter a bit. Which is as nice a job as most of mine."

CHAPTER XX

"Ma's coming, all right!" Montana Marie told Betty gleefully, a week or so after the elopement that didn't come off. "I told her it might be her last chance at a Harding commencement, and she thinks that means that I'm to be in gay Paree with her again next winter, so she's in a very good humor. I hope it's ripping hot weather for commencement. Hot weather wilts Ma right down, and makes her easier to manage."

A few days later Marie had another announcement to make. "Pa is coming East too. Georgia addressed her invitation to Mr. and Mrs. James J., just out of politeness. Now she is wild on the question of tickets for things. If Pa really comes here, her sister Constance will have to go on standing room to the senior play and the Ivy concert. For my part I'm crazy to see Pa, but I don't imagine he'll care much about these commencement doings. His real reason for coming East is to hire an architect in New York —I don't know what he's going to build, but I wrote right back and told him about your friend Mr. Watson." Marie giggled amiably. " That address that Mrs. Hinsdale gave me is forever coming in handy."

Betty wished, quite unreasonably, that Marie's memory for addresses was shorter, or her interest in Jim's career less personal. Whatever Mr. O'Toole meant to build, it would probably be built in Montana ; and Montana is a very, very long way from Harding. It was much nicer having Jim in New York.

Meanwhile Betty was far too busy to spend much thought on the O'Toole family's affairs ; when Mrs. O'Toole actually appeared on the scene, it would be time enough for bothering with her. 19—'s third year reunion was equally imminent and much more interesting. Of course the members who lived in Harding were depended upon to attend to all such details as boarding places and class supper, to plan for informal " stunt-meetings," and to arrange a reunion costume that should go far ahead of that worn by any other returning class. Besides all this, the B. C. A.'s had decided to give a party for 19—. Madeline had glibly agreed to plan it, and had got as far as confiding to all her friends that this time she had really thought of something extra-specially lovely, when the Coach and Six took her to New York, and Agatha Dwight's interest in the fairy play kept her there. At first the B. C. A.'s waited hopefully for her return. Then they held a solemn conclave to discuss their dilemma. But the only plans they could evolve seemed so prosaically commonplace beside Madeline's most casual inspirations that they continued to wait, this time with the calmness born of despair. For the B. C. A. invitations had been sent out broadcast to all 19—ers, and though 19— could have an absurdly good time over "just any old thing," it wasn't "just any old thing" that they would expect of the B. C. A.'s. Finally Betty wrote to Roberta Lewis, who would be passing through New York on her way up to Harding. "Capture Madeline," she ordered summarily. "Bring her up here if you can, but anyway make her tell you about the B. C. A. party. Don't come away without her plans for it, on penalty of being put out of the Merry Hearts—almost."

Luckily for Roberta, Madeline was easily captured. She was sulking in solitary state in her studio apartment, because, though Agatha Dwight liked the fairy play tremendously, no manager could be found to put it on.

"They say, 'Stick to your old line,'" grumbled Madeline. "As if the one play I've written—about a modern woman—was a line. They say, 'New York doesn't care for fairies.' As if every sensible person wasn't born caring for fairies—the really-truly mystic sprites like mine. Oh, I suppose the thing's not good enough! Anyway I won't grumble about it any more. I'll plan a B. C. A. party that will make dear old 19— laugh itself sick. Not a fairy party—a—a germ party, Roberta. You shall be the Ph. D. Germ—in an Oxford gown with a stunning scarlet hood. I shouldn't wonder if Miss Ferris will lend you hers. Then there'll be the Love Germ, and the Wedding Bells Germ, the Club Germ, the Society Germ, and the Germ of a Career. And little Betty Wales shall be the college girl that they

all viciously attack. It shall be a play with
a moral,—one of nice old Mary's nice little
morals. And the moral shall be: 'It isn't
the Germ you like that gets you; it's the
Germ you can't live without.' Could you
imagine life without a Ph. D., Roberta? If
you could, then the modern microbes are still
fighting their hardest for you, and the Love
Germ will get you yet if you don't watch out.
But Betty is the ideal object for the attack of
the modern microbes, because she's a little of
everything, except possibly clubs. Whereas,
the Society microbe wouldn't look at you,
Roberta. It would run away at your ap-
proach."

"Will you come up to Harding to-morrow?" asked Roberta anxiously, ignoring the
aspersion upon her ability to be a society but-
terfly.

"This afternoon if you like," Madeline returned, as calmly as if she hadn't been im-
plored by every mail for two weeks past to
come up and help with the reunion arrangements.

The B. C. A. party turned out a Merry
Hearts' party. Roberta Lewis made a beauti-

ful Ph. D. microbe, with her hair "scrunched back" under a mortar board, big spectacles, and a manner copied from an astronomy instructor who was universally known in Harding circles as Miss Prunes and Prisms. Roberta hadn't acted since the senior play, she said, but she was in splendid form nevertheless. So was K., who, as the Pedagogic Microbe, delivered a speech founded on her personal experiences that brought down the house.

"You must each make up her own part," Madeline told the cast, when they met for the first (and only) rehearsal. "I haven't had time to write out the speeches. Babbie, you ought to know how to lobby for the society act. You liked it pretty well that first winter you were out of college. Eleanor, you're in love; well, explain the sensation. Babe, you don't act as if marriage was a failure; speak up for it. Nita, you're not a really energetic club-woman, I'm happy to say, so here are some few ideas to help you out. I shall speak of a career from bitter experience. Betty, all you have to do is to look thoughtful while we talk, and scared while we fight for you. At the end, when we decide to give you your choice, you are to explain that, since the world is too full of a number of things,— namely modern microbes,—the thing to do is to shut your eyes and decide which one you can't live without. And until you've decided, you propose to enjoy life all around. See? I'll write out your speech, if I can get time, because it ought to be exactly right, to get the best effect. Fire away now, Roberta."

The rehearsal proceeded amid wild confusion. Madeline coolly advised the cast to improve their lines, reminded them encouragingly that the costumes would help out wonderfully, and departed, to compose a new ploshkin song, while the supper committee, to whom she had promised it weeks before, waited patiently on her door-steps to seize and carry it to the printer.

The B. C. A. party was sandwiched in between a thunder-shower and the Glee Club's commencement concert. The stage was an elm-shaded bank, the audience room as much of the adjacent back-campus as would hold 19—, and a few stray specimens of its fiancés, its husbands, and its babies. The "show" was cheered to the echo, and the "eats" which followed, carefully selected from the Tally-ho's latest and most popular specialties, were voted as good as the show.

"Of course," the supper committee chanted, besieging Madeline while she ate, "of course we want it repeated with the class supper stunts."

Madeline waved them away with a spoonful of strawberry ice.

"Talk to the cast. This is one piece of idiocy that I'm not responsible for. Oh, I helped plan it, and I wrote the moral. That's positively all I did. Congratulate K. and Roberta, not me. And have it again for class supper if you really want it. Couldn't we run in the class animals for a sort of chorus— 'Beware the Love Germ, 19—ers,' and so on. Ploshkins and Red Lions, and Jabberwocks and Ritherums would make a lovely Moralizing Chorus. Yes, I'll write it, but I won't make wings for any more animals. I've decided that I'm too old and too distinguished to make any more animals' wings."

19—'s class supper was at the Tally-ho—of course. T. Reed had brought little T. to the reunion, and little T. had brought his big ploshkin mascot to the supper. The undistinguished Mary Jones and her plain, frizzle-haired little girl were there with the class loving-cup. All the old cliques and crowds were there, sitting as they used to sit, but fused, by the esprit de corps that no class had quite so strongly as 19—, into a big, splendid, happy whole. Eleanor was toast-mistress again. It was once toast-mistress, toast-mistress forever, with 19—. Jean Eastman had a speech called "Over the Wide, Wide World," all about wintering in Egypt and buying rugs in Persia and yachting in the strange South Seas. T. Reed had one on "Such is Life," all about raising babies and mushrooms and woolly lambs on a ranch in Arizona. Nita's was called, on the menu-card, "Keep your eye on the Ball," and it was a funny muddle of all the finest things that 19—ers had done by everlasting keeping at it. Roberta's degree was one of the fine things, and Christy's fellowship; and Madeline's play was the grand climax, only Madeline spoiled the rhetorical effect by calling out, "Nita, you know I always do things by not keeping at them. I hereby refuse to point your moral and adorn your tale."

In the midst of Nita's speech Betty Wales disappeared. The few girls who saw her go thought that she was modestly trying to escape hearing her praises sounded by Nita, as one of the people 19— was proudest of. Helen Adams, who had noticed Nora come in and speak to Betty, thought that some domestic crisis demanded her attention, and hoped she wouldn't have to stay in the kitchen very long. For Helen had a speech herself by and by, and she had planned to get through it by looking right into Betty's intent, encouraging little face. But Betty didn't get back in time for Helen's toast nor for the two that came after it. The stunt-doers were gathering in Flying Hoof's stall to put on their costumes, and the rest of the girls were pushing back their chairs to face the platform that Thomas the door-boy had built in front of the fireplace, when Betty Wales got back. She looked as if the domestic crisis had been of a strenuous sort, but at last happily terminated. Her face was flushed, and her hair curled in little damp rings on her forehead. But her expression was as serene as possible, her eyes sparkled with fun, and her dimples just wouldn't stay in, though she tried to be duly serious over having lost half the toasts—and half the supper too.

"But the stunts haven't begun, have they? Does ours come first? Did any engaged girls run around the table that we don't know about already? Little Alice Waite! Oh, how nice! Don't begin our stunt just yet. I want to speak to Madeline a minute. Oh, well, never mind, if they're all waiting."

So the "College Girl and the Modern Microbes, with a Moralizing Chorus of Class Beasts," went at once on the boards. Betty Wales was no actress; not even her warmest admirers had ever imagined that she possessed histrionic ability, and it was only to satisfy a whim of Madeline's that she had taken what she laughingly dubbed "a regular stick part" in the Germ play. But at the class supper performance she surprised everybody by her vivacity. She informed the Ph. D. Germ that she'd better take a course in doing her hair becomingly. She mocked the Pedagogic Germ with the hated epithet "Schoolma'am! schoolma'am!" She caught the Love Germ by an insecure white wing, and assured it

"I'VE SHUT MY EYES AND I'VE CHOSEN"

that nobody fell in love with girls who were just pinned together. All through the contest of the Germs for her she kept interjecting remarks in a disconcertingly unexpected fashion. And at last the time came for the moral. Betty hesitated just a minute, and then began her one regular speech. She began it just as usual, and she went on just as usual until she came almost to the end: "So the thing to do is to shut your eyes and decide which one you can't do without." At this point she shut her eyes for an impressive moment. Then she opened them, and, with a half-frightened, half-merry look at Madeline, she walked up to the Love Germ and the Wedding Bells Germ, and dragged them, one on each side of her, to the front of the platform.

" And so I've shut my eyes and I've chosen, and—please everybody congratulate me quick ! Eleanor Watson first, please, Eleanor dear."

Betty Wales ran down from the platform, still dragging the winning Germs after her, and followed by a riotous mob of other Germs and Class Animals, which was speedily joined by another mob of all the finest class of 19—.

There were no more stunts that night. When the supper committee stopped trying to get a chance to congratulate Betty and hear how it all happened, why, by that time it was much too late for stunts. It was time—and long past time—for the class march to the other suppers, to return serenades and congratulations, and then to visit "Every Loved Spot on the Whole Blessed Campus," as the new ploshkin song put it, and to sing the ploshkin song and the other reunion favorites until everybody was hoarse enough and tired enough to be ready to stop reunioning—and that meant extra-specially hoarse and extra-specially tired; and time in plenty was needed for its accomplishment.

When it was all over, nobody knew anything about Betty's engagement, except that it was to Jim Watson.

"I was out of the room when they ran around the table," she had explained over and over. "So I just spoiled Madeline's lovely moral to tell you. But she says she doesn't mind, and I wanted you all to know, while we're here together, how blissfully happy I am."

" After the rest are out of the way the Merry Hearts will meet in the Peter Pan Annex, top story." So the word went round, when 19— was finally ready to disperse. " The fifteeners went to bed ages ago, so it's empty. We don't want to go to bed."

" I should say not," each Merry Heart acknowledged the news of the rendezvous. " We want to hear all about Betty Wales."

" Yes, Jim came up to-night unexpectedly. Where is he now? In bed, I certainly hope," said Betty Wales. " Ye-es, he'd asked me before, but he never asked me—hard enough. And then Madeline's rule—whether or not you can live without a person—or a thing—is ever so much easier to apply when you're maybe going to lose the person for a long, long time."

" And were you going to lose Jimmie for a long time?" inquired Eleanor, who didn't know any more than the rest how the great desire of her heart—second only to her plans for her own and Dick's happiness—had suddenly become a reality.

Betty nodded proudly. " He's got a splendid big commission. It's to build a town—a whole nice little new town—factories, schools, houses, everything, at a mine and a water power that Mr. O'Toole owns. First he's got to go to Germany to work up some plans for it. It will all take several years. And I saw that I couldn't get along without ——"

"Stop! That's a very dangerous moral," cut in Madeline hastily. " Don't keep repeating it around here, or somebody else may be infected with the Love Germ."

"Very well," agreed Betty gaily, "then I won't say over the dangerous moral. But— the town he has to build is thirty miles from a railroad that hasn't been built. I mean —the town isn't there yet either. And it will be on a railroad by and by, but it isn't now. Wouldn't it be losing Jim pretty hard to have him away off there without me?"

"How about the Coach and Six?" demanded Madeline severely.

Betty went on smiling her happy little smile. "I'll have to start it off somehow before I go. Mr. Morton will understand. He likes Jim. Oh, and when I'm gone there will be a place for Straight. So the twins are settled, and that's one thing off my mind."

"Who'll undertake Montana Marie O'Toole?" demanded Madeline inexorably. "She isn't a thing that you can start off and then leave to go on by herself in proper style."

Betty laughed. "I don't know about that. It's Mr. O'Toole who has commissioned Jim, on Marie's recommendation, to build the town. So she's really responsible about Jim and me. I'm going to tell her to-morrow that, since she can plan things so well for other people, it's time she managed her own affairs better. That is, of course I shall speak to her mother for her, because I promised to. Oh, dear, we can't discuss that, because no one is supposed to know about it yet. But my freshman is all right, anyway."

"I suppose you think the Tally-ho and Morton Hall and the Student's Aid and small Dorothy can get along without you," continued Madeline, who was going to miss Betty dreadfully, and was teasing her to avoid showing her real feelings.

"Of course!" Nothing could daunt Betty Wales to-night. "Anything can get along without anybody—except—Jim and me. Besides, I shall have time to see to all those things before I'm—married. I don't know when Jim is going to Germany. I only saw him for a little minute——"

"Oh!" cried her friends, remembering how many toasts she had missed.

"Well, we didn't get to anything practical like time," Betty defended herself. "But if he has to go too soon, why, we can't be married till he gets home. It takes ages to get ready to be married, doesn't it?" She looked from one to another of the prospective brides, each of whom nodded solemnly. Betty sighed. "I never thought of that. Jim just said that the trip to Germany would be a nice honeymoon. I wonder how soon he has to start. Girls, I really must go to bed. I want to be up early to-morrow morning to talk it all over."

"With us?" demanded Madeline.

"No, human question-point," Betty told her severely. "With Jim."

CHAPTER XXI

THE END OF BETTY WALES

"Wait till I get home from Germany!"
repeated Jim, when he had explained that he
was sailing in ten days, and Betty had explained that getting ready to be married takes
ages and ages. "Never mind a trousseau!
Never mind a linen chest! Never mind even
a wedding dress! Let's just be married.
That's the best way, I think, no matter how
much time you've got. We can run over to
Paris—we shall probably have to anyway—
and you can shop there while I work. You
can do anything you like all the rest of your
life, if you'll only marry me some day next
week. Honestly now, Betty, do you care
about the fuss of weddings?"

"N-o," confessed Betty hesitatingly. "I
guess not. I'm rather tired just now of all
kinds of fuss and complications and crowds."

"Then will you marry me some day next

week ? " asked Jim again with his broadest, most persuasive smile.

" Yes, I will," said Betty Wales, and that matter was definitely settled.

" I think ends are frightful," Betty confided to Madeline, who was helping her pack up on the day after commencement. " I'm glad I've got to hurry, because it will soon be over—the end of Betty Wales. Ends are frightful, because you have to finish everything up just so. No more chances to try again, or smooth things over, or change to something else. And a messy person like me has so many silly little odds and ends to attend to."

"Such as?" queried Madeline, absently packing a brass candlestick on top of Betty's best hat.

Betty rescued the hat skilfully. " Since I'm not going to have any bride things to speak of I must save what I've got," she explained. " Oh, odds and ends like seeing that the shy, homely girls on the summer employment list get positions right away, because the new secretary mightn't think they were good for much ; and seeing that Emily Davis isn't putting herself out too much by staying on

for a while to coach Georgia ; and trimming
Nora's little niece's hat, as I've done every
summer, until she's gotten to depend on it ;
and saying good-bye to the Stocking Factory
people that I know best ; and—oh, dozens of
silly little things like those."

" Incidentally you've got to decide on a
wedding day, haven't you ? "

" Oh, yes," said Betty easily. " That is, I
wrote to Mother to choose any day she pre-
ferred the week after Babbie's. I'm too busy
to think, and the day really doesn't matter. It's going to be at our Lakeside cottage,
you know,—on the big back piazza, I guess,
because that's the prettiest, biggest room in
the house."

A few minutes later a maid brought a telegram to Betty : " Lakeside cottage burned
down last night. How about that impromptu
wedding ? Will Wales."

" Gracious, what a mess ! " exclaimed Betty,
and looked very sober for at least three minutes. Then she smiled again. " I'm glad
that the cottage burned down now, if it had to
burn at all. Lakeside is so dreadfully sandy,
and now that we haven't any house at all, I can

just as well be married in the very place that
I've always wanted to go to a wedding in.
I can stay here quietly with Dorothy, except
when I rush off to Babbie's, and Nan can
come up from Boston a lot easier than she can
go to Cleveland, and Mother and Father and
Will can come here as well as not. They've
never seen the Tally-ho, and they ought to,
before it stops being a little speck mine. And
so I can be married in that little glade in
Paradise—the one that widens out from the
narrow path that looks like an aisle."

"How lovely!" cried Madeline eagerly.
"I should think that was nicer than any cottage! And the bridal party and the guests
can go in boats—so much more romantic
than carriages or motor-cars."

"And the wedding feast can be a picnic,"
laughed Betty. "Bob will be extra-specially
delighted with that idea."

"And the music——" began Madeline,
when the maid interrupted again. This time
it was callers.

"A lady and a gentleman," Maggie explained. "They didn't give no names."

"The tribe of O'Toole," Madeline guessed

gaily, "come to reproach you for your prospective abandonment of their offspring, and
for having let Straight Dutton give her that
dreadful dictionary of slang. Her conversation is a mass of quotations from it."

"Oh, dear, I hope they won't be cross about
anything," sighed Betty, starting for the door.

"If they are, call me. I'll finish them in
short order," Madeline promised savagely.

Betty was gone a long time, but she did not
send for Madeline, who, forgetting that the
new wedding arrangement would defer packing, continued to pile candlesticks upon hats
and to stuff Betty's fresh shirt-waists into her
chafing dish and her copper teakettle, to save
room. Finally a lazy mood fell upon her, and
she curled up on Betty's cushioned window-
seat, to think about the picnic-wedding—how
she would trim the bride's boat, and what
would be the very nicest "eats" for a wedding
feast in a wood. It was to be a Wedding
Feast, with capitals, Madeline decided; calling it a picnic took away the novelty and the
dignity of the occasion.

"What do you think?" began Betty Wales,
breaking excitedly into Madeline's medita-

tions. "What do you think has happened now, Madeline Ayres?"

"Paradise hasn't burned up too, has it?" asked Madeline lazily. "Because I'm planning the loveliest features for a Paradise wedding."

"Don't be silly, Madeline." Betty ungratefully ignored the promised features.

"Well, have the O'Tooles persuaded you that it's a fatal mistake for you to abandon Montana Marie?"

"Please don't be silly," Betty reiterated. "It's nothing about the wedding or about me. It's about Harding. Mr. O'Toole is just splendid, Madeline. He's quick-tempered and short-spoken like Mr. Morton, but he's awfully nice. And he's going to give Harding—well, it's not decided what, but something perfectly splendid."

"Oh, was that why President Wallace was so interested in your freshman?"

"Certainly not," said Betty, with much dignity. "But I know now why President Wallace was so anxious to have her get through successfully. You know there was a lot of trouble about her entering Harding, and

Mrs. O"Toole kept on insisting, because she hates to have Marie disappointed in anything. She had always bought things for her before, so she tried to buy her a chance to enter Harding without entrance conditions or any worries of that kind. Of course President Wallace refused, but he was sorry for Marie and he let her in, as he sometimes has other exceptional girls, on condition that she should keep her work strictly up to the standard. Then he was naturally anxious for her to succeed, both for her own sake and to show her mother that honest work and not money are the requirements of this college. Mr. O"Toole understood all that. He was dreadfully annoyed when he heard what his wife had done. He says if he had been President Wallace he'd have just 'sent those fool women-folk flying.' He thinks President Wallace has done a lot for Marie, and now he wants to 'square up,' as he calls it. He wants me to suggest what Harding needs, and to explain to President Wallace that this gift is entirely different from Mrs. O'Toole's offer. That won't be hard, since Marie is going to leave."

"Is she?" cried Madeline, making a wry

face. "Just as I'd definitely decided to use her for the heroine of my next novel!"

"Mrs. O'Toole has decided that she cares less about a title in the family than about Marie's being happy, and as Marie never had any trouble in deciding what she couldn't live without, she's going to marry a nice man from Montana just as soon as she can get ready. Next fall, I suppose that will be."

"She's been rather amusing," reflected Madeline, "if she has bothered a lot at times."

Betty stared, wide-eyed, at this wrong-headed view of things. "She never meant to bother. And she was the one who made me decide about Jim."

Madeline laughed gleefully. "I wondered how long you'd keep on talking as if splendid gifts to Harding College were your chief interest in life, Betty Wales. By the way, speaking of tea-shops, has Mr. Morton answered your letter?"

"He telegraphed," Betty explained. "He just said, 'He's a nice boy, Miss B. A., and you can manage him, so I wish you much joy.' Not a word about the Coach and Six. I hope he isn't hurt at my backing out. Do you think he can be, Madeline?"

For answer Madeline picked her small friend up and tucked her in among the cushions of the window-seat. "You are not to worry about people's feeling hurt," she ordered. "People will feel sorry, of course—foolish people like me. I have an idea that I'm going to miss you fearfully, Betty Wales. A career is an awfully lonely thing, the week your very best little pal is getting married. But you've always been true to your title. You've been Miss B. A. to Mr. Morton and to every single other soul you've ever had anything to do with. That's why we're bound not to lose you now, for all of Jim."

"You dear old Madeline! As if Jim or I wanted to lose our dearest friends! Now tell me about the wedding-with-features, so I can write it all to Mother, and then she won't mind so much about the cottage. And help me think of some splendid gifts to suggest to President Wallace, so I can see him to-day, and then write to Mr. O'Toole that it's all arranged. And help me to try on my bridesmaid's dress for Babbie's wedding, to be sure if it fits. See how I can't get along without you, you dear silly Madeline!"

"That's one way to say it," Madeline told her, "but the truth is —— Oh, stop me, somebody! If I get to sentimentalizing over the happy past I shall weep, and with a rapid succession of festal occasions looming before me I can't spare a handkerchief so early in the game."

The day of the Paradise wedding-with-features was a made-to-order feature in itself. The sun sparkled on the water. A tricksy little wind rippled the waves, and ruffled the leaves of Paradise wood. In the deep, still glades the thrushes sang like mad. The bride's boat, from edge to water-line, was a mass of fine white "bridal wreath" blossoms. The groom's boat was decked with laurel. The guests sat among daisy-wreaths. Somewhere in the wood human musicians were hidden, and their notes came faint and far and fairylike in the pauses of the thrushes' concert. Betty's soft white dress didn't, as K. said, look a bit "wedding-i-fied." She looked like a sweet spring flower, against the shadowy green of the wedding aisle, down which she came with her father, the Smallest Sister leading the way, proud and anxious and much excited, in her capacity of solitary attendant. There were no bridesmaids, because Betty hadn't been able to choose among the Merry Hearts.

" And if I have them all," she said, " why, there'll be more bridesmaids than wedding guests."

Madeline had superintended the roping-off of the chosen glade with daisy-chains, and bunches of daises tied to the branches of the trees at one end made a blossomy background for the bridal party to stand against.

"Oh, it takes such a little minute to be married!" cried Betty Wales in an awestruck voice, when it was over.

" It's going to take time to eat the Wedding Feast," Madeline announced, and led the way down a little side path to the water's edge. There the Wedding Feast was spread on a long table, lovely with ferns and more daisies. Bridget and Nora were in charge, but under them worked a small army of water-nymphs, dryads, elves, and woodland fairies, who seated the guests and then served them, giving odd, fairy names to prosaic dishes, and pausing in their labors to dance, sing, and chant the Lay of the Woodland Wedding, which Madeline and Helen Adams had sat up the whole night before Babbie's wedding to compose, as an engagement present for Betty Wales. The nymphs, elves, and fairies were professors' small sons and daughters, not yet off on their vacations, and Stocking Factory children from the other hill—all as merry and companionable together as possible. Mary Brooks Hinsdale and Emily Davis had dressed them, according to Madeline's orders. Georgia Ames had taught them the songs and the Woodland Wedding Lay, and Bob, who had learned a lot of folk-dances at a New York settlement, came up two days early to contribute her share to the Loveliest Wedding.

That was what Mary christened it, as the wedding party took ship again ; and Mary's names always stuck.

" Oh, it is, of course," agreed Babbie, a little wistfully. She and Mr. Thayer had planned their journeyings to include Betty's wedding. " And the most impromptu. It makes even yours seem quite cold and formal, Mary."

"For once," put in Bob placidly, "I've eaten as much wedding cake as I wanted. Picnics are the only time you can eat all you want, you know, and still be a perfect lady. That's why I particularly adore them."

Up at Morton Hall Jasper J. Morton, who had come to the wedding with Babe and John, was berating them both roundly because he had forgotten most of his present for Betty— the part he had remembered was merely a wonderful old silver tea-service fit for a princess.

"Oh, well, it's no matter," he acknowledged at last. "Nothing to boil over at, Miss B. A. It's very easy to describe the missing articles — a deed to the Coach and Six and to my share in the Tally-ho. Conditioned on your dining with me once every time you come to New York to look after your properties."

Betty gasped. "Oh, Mr. Morton, you shouldn't give me anything more. It isn't right to give two—three wedding presents. Such splendid ones, too!"

Mr. Morton smiled at her fondly. "You've given me lots of presents, Miss B. A.,—a kind friend, a keen critic, a cure-all for bad temper and impatience, and a teacher of all the fun there is in life, the real fun that doesn't depend on 'doing' the other fellow in business. Besides, Miss B. A., about that tea-shop now. I'm a selfish old man. I don't want a tea-shop, and I do want to hang on to you. I'm interested in your business theories." He chuckled. " I want you to keep on discovering 'em. I'm glad you're Mrs. Jim Watson "—Betty jumped at the strange new name—" but I'll wager young Watson here doesn't want you to settle down into just Mrs. Jim. It'll do you good to have a tea-shop to think about sometimes. Not to worry about, mind you ; the Coach and Six is on a sound business basis. And remember, Miss B. A., there's one thing I haven't changed about. I always did perfectly hate to be thanked."

" Then I shan't try," laughed Betty. " And I shan't let you off one of those dinners. I shall love having the tea-shops. It makes me feel less as if this was the end of Betty Wales —less as if I'd been blown out to make room for Mrs. Jim." Betty made a funny little face at Jim, who retorted with, " Haven't forgotten that train, have you, Mrs. Jim? "

When the carriage came for them, the elves and wood fairies surrounded it and pelted the bridal couple with armfuls of daisies instead of rice and old shoes. So it was through a rain of daisies that Betty caught her last glimpse of the Merry Hearts, who stood in a little group by themselves waving her off.

"Good-bye, Betty Wales."

"Good-bye, Mrs. Jim."

> " Here's to Betty 'n Jim, drink 'em down,
> Here's to Betty 'n Jim, drink 'em down,
> Here's to Betty 'n Jim,
> She is very fond of him,
> Drink 'em down, drink 'em down, drink 'em down,
>   down, down!"

The carriage had rounded the curve in the road, but the Merry Hearts still stared after it in rather somber silence.

"Just the same——" Madeline broke the pause disconsolately. "Just the same, it is the end of Betty Wales."

"Yes," agreed Eleanor chokingly.

"Certainly it is," put in Mary Brooks decisively. "And high time, in my opinion. Do you want her to wear herself out doing things for other people, with nobody whose special business it is to do things for her? Do you want her to miss any of the good things life has for her? I say, hurrah for Montana Marie O'Toole, who helped Betty decide on Jim."

"That's right, Mrs. Hinsdale," broke in Mr. Morton excitedly. "I've been doing my best for some time, but I guess I'm a poor hand at matchmaking. Anyhow it took the young lady from Montana to pull this affair off."

"Things were so nice as they were," mourned Madeline.

"They're terribly nice as they are, I think," said little Helen Adams eagerly.

"Hurrah for the end of Betty Wales!" cried Bob.

"Hurrah for Betty Wales herself!" put in Madeline.

"Hurrah for Mrs. Jim!" shouted all the Merry Hearts together, so loudly that Betty and Jim, who had stopped the carriage just around the curve to shake off the daisies, heard it and smiled appreciatively at each other.

"And for Mr. Jim!" went on the chorus

impartially. "And for their married life!" it ended, to round out the subject.

Betty snuggled closer to Jim. "It's all been lovely, and I shall like having the tea-shops to remind me of old times, but I like most extra-specially much being just Mrs. Jim."

"And I like more extra-specially than I can say having you for Mrs. Jim," her husband told her.

"Then everything is extra-specially all right, isn't it?" said Betty Wales Watson, with a happy little smile.

CPSIA information can be obtained at www.ICGtesting.com
Printed in the USA
BVOW04s0510101213

338615BV00001BA/78/P